Also by Stephen Potts

Hunting Gumnor

Tommy Trouble

COMPASS MURPHY

STEPHEN POTTS

Mammoth

For and from Endeavour

First published in Great Britain in 2001
by Mammoth, an imprint of Egmont Children's Books Ltd
a division of Egmont Holding Limited
239 Kensington High Street, London W8 6SA

Text copyright © 2001 Stephen Potts
Cover illustration copyright © 2001 Mark Preston

The moral rights of the author and cover illustrator
have been asserted

ISBN 0 7497 4027 2

10 9 8 7 6 5 4 3

A CIP catalogue record for this title is available from
the British Library

Typeset by Avon DataSet Ltd, Bidford on Avon, Warks.
www.avondataset.com
Printed and bound in Great Britain by Cox & Wyman Ltd,
Reading, Berkshire

Part 1
Waiting in Whitby

Chapter 1

Joshua shivered. Maybe it was just the cold, but something in the way the mist pooled, moonlit and milky, in the hollow below, made him uneasy. He whistled the dog closer to his side, huddled deeper into his coat, and followed the path down.

He hurried head-bowed through the hollow, as fast as his footing allowed. Wet flints glistened slickly in the sucking mud, as he slipped and slithered past, brushing veils of moisture-beaded cobwebs from the bushes. It was only when he broke through to the clear air of Beacon Hill on the up-side beyond, that he realised he'd been holding his breath. He let it go in a gasp. The dog glanced up at this. Joshua patted its nose and looked around. Just below the summit, where the grass grew long in the gorse fringes, were what he knew he'd find here tonight. 'Told, you, Nelson, didn't I?' he said.

Two ewes, each with a singleton lamb, stared wide-eyed at him and the dog. A third ewe nearby ignored them, and instead nuzzled a lamb which lay slumped in the damp grass. Beyond them all, to the north, a luminous smudge swept the horizon, where the lighthouse beam lit up the clouds behind the summit.

Joshua bent to the trembling creature. Its rapid breath blew warm on his hand when he lifted it to its feet. It staggered briefly on legs like fish, then fell in an ungainly heap, bleating thinly. He'd have to take this one back to the farm. He unbuttoned his coat and tucked the lamb inside, then set off back down, with its anxious mother following close by. The other sheep, more mindful of the dog, lagged behind.

Suddenly Nelson stopped. He lowered his head and raised his hackles, and a low growl rumbled in his throat. Joshua bade him hush and listened hard. The night was still and cold, and sound seemed to magnify. He could hear the breakers on the cliff-foot, and an owl-hoot in the wood, but there was nothing in that to alarm a

4

dog. Nelson growled again, and this time Joshua heard it too. There was someone in the hollow, heading this way. Someone big.

Joshua stiffened. He couldn't tell if the turmoil under his coat was the lamb's shivers or his own hammering heart. A tall dark figure emerged from the mist, striding towards him. Nelson barked fiercely and leapt forward. Joshua winced, waiting for the sounds of conflict and pain, but all he heard were excited yelps and all he could see was the black and white blur of Nelson's tail. Then came a voice he knew better than his own. 'All right, Nelson. England expects, eh? Good dog.'

'Father!' cried Joshua, startling the lamb. The dark shape drew up and stooped to him. 'Well, lad,' he grinned. He laid one hand on Joshua's shoulder, and ran the other over the lamb's head where it peered out of his coat. His expression clouded when he saw Joshua's shivers. 'Why, you're frozen, son,' he said. 'And hungry too, I'll warrant.' Joshua nodded.

His father straightened, shaking his head. 'While them indoors sup broth by t' fire.' He held out his hand. 'Here, son, I'll take t' beast.'

Joshua declined. 'No, father. He warms me as much as I do him.' This was more than he'd said for the past two days, since his father had left for the herring-boats at Whitby. He wasn't due back till Sunday. Why was he up here tending him while he tended sheep?

They had to single file back through the hollow, but on the upper meadow beyond, Joshua drew alongside. 'Father?' he ventured.

His father guessed his query, and stilled it with a hand on his back. 'Later, son. When you're warmed and fed. Ask me then.' And they headed on down to the farm lights.

Joshua sat opposite his father at the heavy table, enjoying the warm glow of the high-banked fire behind him. At his feet Nelson nagged and gnawed at a cattle bone he could never quite grip with his forepaws.

A thin woman with long dark hair approached the table. 'More broth, Thomas?' she asked.

Joshua's father nodded. 'If you will please, Esther, yes.' When she reached for his bowl he grasped her arm with a powerful hand and fixed her firmly with his gaze. 'But first the lad, eh? He has more need than I.'

Joshua's bowl stood empty, wiped clean by the heavy brown bread. He was still hungry, yes, but he didn't want trouble, not if his father was going away. Aunt Esther looked first at his father as he released his grip, then across at the silent man in the fireplace chair. She turned back and flicked a quick thin smile from father to son. 'Of course, Thomas. That he has, judging by yon bowl. Here, lad.' She took the bowls and filled them from the great pot hanging over the fire. The silent man had to move his legs to let her by. Joshua saw him scowl.

By the time he'd finished his second bowl, Joshua was warmed through, and drowsiness crept up from his weary legs. His father saw this and stood up. 'Time for some sleep, son. Come on, I'll help.' He reached for the carefully tied bed-roll stowed behind the scullery door, and smiled when he picked it up. 'Neat as ever, I see.'

Esther cleared the bowls to the sink, and Joshua caught her eye as he got down from the table. 'Good night, Aunt Esther,' he said. She slipped a last crust into his hand. They both looked at the silent man who'd been staring into the fire ever since Joshua and his father returned. He hadn't noticed. 'Good night, Mr Flint,' offered Joshua. The only reply was a grunt.

Through in the scullery his father was already untying the lashings on the bed-roll. There were seven of them, evenly spaced along the grey canvas cloth. Joshua changed into his nightshirt and folded his clothes neatly on to the single chair, listening while his father ran through the familiar list of the seven seas, and untied a lashing for each. 'North Atlantic . . . South Atlantic . . . Southern.' Nelson came in, minus his bone, and settled with a sigh on his patch of sackcloth. 'North Pacific . . . South Pacific . . . Indian.' Joshua stared at his father. He'd changed the order. It could only mean one thing.

There was a long pause, while his father gathered into his voice as much warmth as he could muster for such a cold name: 'Arctic.' Joshua turned away to hide his welling tears. He bent to stroke Nelson's head while his father slung the hammock from the bars he'd fitted to the ceiling beams years before, when they had first moved in. Thomas lifted his son with his huge harpooneer hands and swung him into the hammock. Then he unfolded two heavy and much-patched blankets from the chest by the chair, and spread them over his son, tucking them in at his shoulders. Joshua sniffed. The single candle showed a sparkling dampness in his eyes.

His father tousled the curly brown hair. 'It's the last time, son. I promise. Then it'll be you and me together, in a place of our own. Just one more trip.'

Joshua said nothing. It wasn't that he begrudged his father his time in the north, for he had spoken of it so often, and in such tones of awe, that Joshua could see the arctic scenes whenever he closed his eyes and willed up the pictures his father had conjured. He envied his father for having been to such a place, and part of him was glad he would see it again. But a season in the ice seemed so impossibly long, and back here in Whitby Joshua would be at the mercy of an unrestrained Flint. And then there were the risks: the storms, the icebergs, the bears, and, worst of all, the ever-present spectre of a dwindling death through scurvy and starvation should the ship be frozen fast in the endless polar night.

But the picture his father painted now was a warmer one. When he returned in the autumn, enriched by his exploits, they could at last have a farmhouse to themselves. There'd be a big hearth, with an inglenook seat, for stories. And upstairs, a real bed in a real bedroom. He couldn't take Nelson but he'd have a dog that was truly his. Maybe two. They'd work their own fields and tend their own beasts together; and then, the farmwork done, they'd go fishing from the rocks or in a borrowed boat.

The brightness in his father's eye, and the warmth in his voice, revealed to Joshua how much he too wanted to believe in the future he described, and Joshua knew that he had to let him go. He took a deep breath, then spoke, softly but steadily.

'I will wait for you, Father, and while I wait I will hope for these better things.' At these words a strange look flitted briefly over his father's well-weathered face, but it was soon chased away as Joshua went on. 'But come back safe, and come back soon.' Joshua closed his eyes, lest his father see more tears.

It was his father's turn to say nothing now. He stood in silence, gently swinging the hammock until he was sure Joshua had fallen asleep, then snuffed the candle and quietly closed the door.

Chapter 2

Any sleep Joshua managed was fitful, and broken by dreams more vivid than usual. His hammock floated free, in a clean silvery sky above an impossibly flat sea. Somehow he knew that he was flying north, drifting past towering clouds, which solidified as he neared them into great canyons of ice. Below, under the water, huge shadowy fish-shaped creatures were dimly visible, their black and white forms moving with a silent but threatening grace. A much smaller but also black and white animal approached, running across the surface of the sea. The hammock swept wildly downwards until Joshua recognised Nelson by the pattern of his patches. He was running, not on water, but on ice: an enormous featureless sheet of it, stretching to the horizon in all directions.

A sudden violent blow shook the ice from below, closely followed by another. The creatures beneath were hurling themselves upwards at their icy ceiling, again and again, until it began to fracture. If these were whales they were hunters, not hunted. The ice nearby splintered, and a monstrous head broke through. It fixed upon Joshua and his dog with tiny malevolent eyes. Hundreds of teeth glinted in its cruel mouth. It dropped back through the ice and gathered to ram upwards again, directly beneath them. Nelson yelped in fear.

Joshua woke with a start. His hammock was swinging with his restlessness, and below him Nelson, dog-dreaming, twitched and yelped. Through the wall voices were raised. He heard his father and Mr Flint, and although he did not hear her speak, he knew Aunt Esther too was present.

'And if you're frozen in?' Flint demanded.

'We won't be.' Joshua sensed his father's efforts to stay calm.

'Two ships were, last winter.' Joshua tensed. He didn't know this.

'Two of twenty-five. And all returned safe, with a good catch.'

'But I need more than assurance. There have been dry years too, in your time and mine, when ships have slipped home with not one whale in the hold.'

There was a long pause. Joshua heard footsteps, then the turning of a key in a little-used lock. His father's voice, when it came, had a heaviness to it. 'Here. It's all I have. That'll keep him the whole summer, and half the winter beyond. *If* we're frozen in. T' rest can come in arrears.'

There was another pause, filled with the clink of counted coins. 'This will do till Candlemas next,' said Flint. 'And he'll have to work.'

There was a thump on the table. It sounded like a whalehead against underfoot ice. 'Was he not working tonight?' his father shouted. Nelson stirred and woke. 'While you supped? And his cousins warm in their beds?'

Chair legs scraped on the flagstone floor as someone stood up. 'It's not as if he's kin to me,' shouted Flint, just as loud.

Esther spoke at last, urging them both to hush. 'Enough of this. There's children asleep in this house. And all of them are kin to *me*.' A chair creaked as Flint sat back down. Esther continued. 'Thomas, you must know that half the time t' moor is where Joshua *chooses* to be. He's like a ghost at table when he's here and he says more to yon dog than any one of us. It's as if he prefers the company of beasts and the sky above his head to this, his home and hearth.'

Joshua looked over the lip of the hammock. He sensed, more than saw, Nelson's eyes upon him, and he knew that Esther was right – but not completely. This had *never* been his home.

With his father's help Joshua got through his daily duties much faster than usual, even though his broken night, the shouting, and above all, his father's pending departure weighed down on his shoulders like a pair of overfull milk-pails. By midday they were on to the last job – fetching fodder for the cows. They worked side by side in silence, until at length his father planted his pitchfork in the ground and spoke. 'Well, Joshua, that's us done. The day's bright enough and tides on t' ebb. What say we head up to Saltwick for some shellfish?'

Joshua's load lightened. The sight of mussels or winkles on a plate before him made his stomach churn, however hungry he was – but collecting them was a different matter, especially if it meant time with his dad. 'Can Nelson come?' he asked, eagerly.

Half an hour later man, boy, and dog were

heading north, towards the hollow where they had met the previous night. It looked so different in daylight, and Joshua hurried through, embarrassed to recall his fears. A mile or so beyond they reached the cliff top. The sea spread before them, grey-blue, rumpled, and dotted about with the russet sails of luggers and fishing cobles.

They turned west along the cliff path, and soon came upon the Nabs, two large black outcrops of rock either side of Saltwick Bay. Nearby Black Nab stuck up through the surf like a huge thumb; while the more distant and lower lying Saltwick Nab looked, to Joshua, like a pair of giant's knuckles in a wash day tub of suds. Joshua had always found Black Nab sinister somehow, and more so today, though he couldn't say why. Uneasiness rose within him when he scrambled after his father down the steeply sloping path to the foreshore, under Black Nab's eye. It soon faded again as he set to work with his back to the sea, hunting for mussels, while Nelson padded about in search of seagulls.

Joshua's bag was nearly full when Nelson's barking lifted his head. A pair of gulls flapped lazily away past the Nab while Nelson splashed after them. The wave surge at Black Nab's base made it look as if the rock was driving onshore, directly towards Nelson. Joshua suddenly felt uneasy again, and this time he knew why. 'Father?' he asked. 'The whales you hunt. Are they hunters too?'

His father straightened his back with a wince. 'No, son. Not really. Some on 'em eat squid on t' sea floor, but mostly, big though they are, they strain sea water for specks o' food the size o' breadcrumbs.' He set down his bag of mussels, as shiny and black as the rocks they'd clung to. 'There *are* whales that hunt seal and such. Killers they're called, and right fierce they are too. We steer well clear. You mark 'em by their black and white patches and the big fin on their back, sticking straight up. Like yon rock.' He pointed to Black Nab.

Joshua looked, but not at the rock his father indicated, for over his shoulder he could see the seas roll in and break upon Saltwick Nab behind him. Joshua suddenly saw a whale in this rock, too; a big one, finless, and bound northwards to the open sea. A wave broke against its head, raising a cloud of white spray. 'Thar she blows!' yelled Joshua.

His father turned. When the next wave struck he saw it too – the spout of a great whale, blowing hard. He grinned at Joshua and joined in his game. 'Right, me hearties, let's launch the boats!' he called, and ran off along the water's edge. The whale's tail lay close to shore, and was easily reached, but Nelson, more water-wary, hung back. Waves swept over the whale's lower back, while Joshua watched, counting the seconds between them. He chose his moment and stepped forward warily. Where it was wet the rock was oily, and where it was dry it crumbled. He faced a choice: go carefully and get swamped by the next big wave, or rush ahead and risk slipping down the whale's flanks to the jaggy shards and hungry crabs that lurked beneath the froth. He looked ahead and saw the next big North Sea roller roaring in, and found himself frozen in fear.

Then came a firm hand in his back propelling him onwards and upwards, so that he was launched above the incoming surge, to land a-sprawl on the whale's head. Spray fell around him heavier than any rain he'd ever known. His father laughed. 'Bit off more than you could chew, eh? It's like that wi' real whales sometimes.' He stamped the rock. 'Imagine this thing bucking and heaving and the water about so cold it freezes your hair. Two harpoons in and he's dragging you through icebergs, trying to dive. You pray he tires before he tips you.'

'Don't,' said Joshua. 'Please don't.' He stood

up and walked to the very edge of the rock, staring ahead as if steering the whale northwards and home.

He felt his father's hand on his shoulder. 'I'm sorry, son.' There was a pause. 'I've never been tipped in yet, and I don't mean to start now.'

'Don't leave me alone here,' Joshua said. He'd meant it as a plea to be careful, but his father took it as an entreaty not to go at all.

'They need me, Joshua. They almost begged. Which means they'll pay me so much I need never go again.' He removed his heavy sweater, and undid his flannel shirt. A key hung from a much-weathered string around his neck. He lifted it over his head and held it out. 'I want you to look after this. It opens my chest in Flint's farmhouse. I've sold just about everything we had to pay off the doctors' bills, but there's precious things in there still. Not money precious, but worth the world to me. I want you to look after them and keep them from Flint. He'll sell them soon as look at you. Promise?'

Joshua looked gravely up at his father as he hung the key round his neck. 'Promise,' he said.

'Good lad. Now we'll let this whale go. I've some work to do on't ship, so Nelson can guide you home.'

To the dog's great relief they retraced their

steps to the shore and then up to the cliff path, where they parted. Joshua swung the mussel bags over his shoulder and watched his father head west towards Whitby. He heard snatches of whistling in the wind, and he knew that, whatever his father said, his going to sea again wasn't just about money.

Chapter 3

Joshua blinked in the still half-dark. 'Come on son,' his father whispered in his ear. 'We've a tide to catch.' He was spilled out of his hammock and into his clothes, yawning and bleary. He'd lain awake for hours the night before, waiting for his father to return. The last thing he remembered was the church clock across the fields striking two. And now, not yet dawn, here was his father, wide awake, washed, dressed, and ready to go. How did he do it?

Joshua finished dressing while his father rummaged in the larder for breakfast. The kitchen door creaked open and in stepped Esther. 'I'll do that Thomas,' she said, as she shooed him away. 'You finish packing.'

He turned to his heavy sea-bag on the floor, thick sweaters piled around it. 'Sorry if I woke you.'

'I woke myself. You don't think I'd let a brother of mine ship out without a farewell, do you?'

He smiled and shook his head, then paused in his packing to look at her. 'But what about –'

'He's sleeping. It's better this way.' She laid three plates on the table, and smiled at Joshua as he slid on to his usual seat. 'And don't worry – I'll say goodbye to Laurence and Emmy for you.'

'Thanks, Esther.' He stood up, propped the bag against the wall, and pulled the drawstring tight. It bulged to bursting. 'There. I'm done.'

'What about this?' Esther pointed to a battered knapsack hanging from the door handle. 'Can you manage it all?'

'I'll help,' Joshua piped up.

His father sat down. 'I hadn't meant you to go all the way to town, Joshua. How would you get back on your own?'

Esther ladled out some porridge. 'That's another reason why I'm up, Thomas. Me and Joshua are coming to your ship with you.' Joshua looked up at her. It was the first he'd heard of it, but there was nothing he wanted more.

'Are you sure? There's no need,' said his father.

'Maybe not. But it's what we want. Isn't it, lad?' Joshua nodded vigorously. 'Now sup up the both of you.'

Half an hour later they were walking west to Whitby. The sun was now up, but still low in the sky, casting long shadows before them. Each of the little party bore a burden which gave the shadows strange shapes. Joshua's father slung his sea bag over one shoulder, while beside him Joshua proudly wore the knapsack on his back. Esther, who had told her husband she was off to market, carried a wicker basket full of butter and eggs. Nelson carried nothing but slouched along as if he did. Even as a working dog he was unused to such an early start.

Drowsy though he was, Nelson heard before anyone else the rattle of cartwheels and the clip-clop of hooves on the road behind them. All four of them turned to watch the two-horse cart approach. The driver was bundled up against the early chill, but he was easily recognised as he pulled the horses to a halt. They fidgeted in their traces, puffing great clouds of steam, and eyeing the dog nervously.

'Morning all. A lovely day, what?' said the man in the cart, cheerily.

'Morning, Vicar,' said Esther, with a curtsey.

Joshua's father was cooler. 'Mr Robson,' he said, with the slightest nod of his head.

'To town?' asked the vicar. 'Then we're well met, for I am bound there too. Please ride with me.'

Joshua's father tossed his sea-bag in the back of the cart and climbed up to the driver's bench seat, then stooped to help Esther up. He smiled down at Joshua. 'In t' back with t' dog,' he said.

Joshua took Nelson away from his efforts to outstare the horses, and round to the rear of the cart, where he lifted him in, and clambered up after. He sat on his father's bag, with Nelson securely between his feet. A heavy wooden box lay on either side of him.

'All aboard?' asked the vicar, then twitched the horses into motion with a flick of his whip, and they set off.

'Fine-looking eggs there, Esther,' said the vicar. 'But are you not early for market?'

'Early for market, I'll grant you, but on time for tide,' said Esther. The vicar looked at Joshua's father with a raised eyebrow.

' 'Tis true. I'm Greenland bound.' He didn't look back at the vicar. 'On the *Lindisfarne*.'

'As harpooneer? I thought you were done with that.' Joshua edged back on the bag, the better to hear the two men talk.

'I am. I sail as specksioneer.' Joshua knew this term, though most boys his age did not. On a whaling ship the specksioneer was a foreman among foremen, the head harpooneer, and second only to the captain overall.

'Of course, of course. Poor Darley. A fine man.' The cart rattled on in silence, then the vicar spoke again. 'The cholera lingers yet up at Staithes, I hear.'

'It does, sir.' Another pause. 'She were fully crewed and near set to sail when Darley took ill and died. Rest on t' fleet were long gone, on account o' all t' work she'd needed, so there was none left to call on. Then skipper minded me. There and then, he rowed out to my herring-boat to offer me specksioneer, and such a wage I could say naught but aye. I've been working all hours on her since, and we sail on t' morning tide.'

'I see. Well I must make the tide too. Though not for myself.' He turned to indicate the wooden boxes with a jab of his whip. Joshua had crept so close to listen in he was nearly hit. 'Our old bibles and prayer books. They've seen good service, but we were bought an entire new set last month, so these are off on a coal ship to Jarrow. A mission church there stands in need.'

Silence fell again: Esther speculating on who'd

24

bought the new bibles, Thomas thinking about Darley, whose shoes he was to fill, and Joshua uneasy to hear of this last minute work on his father's ship. Nelson thought about nothing at all.

Mr Robson, who was least comfortable with silence, being so well educated, babbled on. 'I don't think I could have been a sailor, Thomas. Not for the seasickness, or the months away from home. No, this getting up in the middle of the night for a watch, or whatever, would surely have done for me. Still, time and tide wait for no man, as they say.'

Joshua's father tapped one of the boxes behind him. 'Nor, it seems, do they wait for the word of God.'

'Thomas!' exclaimed Esther, shocked to hear him speak this way, and to the vicar, too.

Robson broke the awkward silence which followed. 'It's all right, Esther,' he said to her, 'Thomas and I have talked like this before.' He turned the other way on his driving seat. 'Have we not, Thomas?' There was no response, so he continued. 'God moves in mysterious ways, Thomas, and I pray that one day you will come to see that. I know that you have suffered a grievous loss, but –'

Joshua clapped his hands to his ears and slid forward. Where before he'd wanted to eavesdrop every word, now he sought silence, and the solace that came with it. The cart rattled over the ruts, with the sun still low in his eyes. He felt the turn that told him they were now on the descending road, and soon saw the Abbey ruins behind him, standing stark and unsoftened by the rosy light. The road dropped down past houses standing ever closer-packed, then turned again, on to the quayside where the coal boats lay. The harbour was busy with herring-boats landing their catch, and bigger vessels making ready to sail. Joshua sniffed at the rich mixture of smells wafting past – coal-dust and kipper-smoke foremost among them – as he looked about at the tangled forest of masts and spars, trying to make out the names of the ships. Most were obscured by coal-dust. When the cart finally stopped, he lifted his hands from his head, and heard Mr Robson call to the grimy vessel moored alongside.

'Ahoy there!' he shouted, in a voice very different from the one he used for his Sunday sermons. 'Are you the *Sunderland*?'

A sailor's head popped up from the forward hatch. His eyes stood out white in his coal-blackened face. 'Aye. That we are.'

'Then I have cargo for you.' After more shouting two sailors climbed up to the quay and unloaded the heavy boxes from the cart. They were about to move them on to the ship, when Mr Robson called a halt. He opened the lid of the first box and drew out a battered black book.

'I wish you well, Thomas, and you and your crewmates safe home. Please accept this.' He handed him the book. 'I hope you find some comfort within it.'

They shook hands, then Mr Robson mounted his cart again. 'Must go,' he called, as he sped off. 'Early communion, you know.'

Joshua's father bent down behind him, undid the knapsack he still bore, and slipped the book inside. Then he pointed over Joshua's shoulder, to a ship on the opposite quay. 'There she is, son. Over t' bridge. Doesn't she look grand?'

And she did. Sailors busied about her like ants round their queen. Her paintwork shone brightly, and her brilliant sails lay tightly bundled to the spars, like curtains too new to be drawn. Joshua didn't understand: he knew her to be an old ship, yet here she was decked out like a girl at her first dance.

His father led the way across the rickety draw-bridge, and along the quayside to the *Lindisfarne*'s bow. He was greeted there by other sailors, some already at their work, others arriving like him. Their sea-bags clustered on deck like a company of caterpillars, to be carried below, one by one, down to the heart of their fo'c'sle nest.

Joshua's father dropped to the quarterdeck to confer with the captain, then returned to the quay. 'An hour or so yet,' he said. 'And plenty of work in that time for me. What would you do?'

'I'll to t' market-place,' said Esther. 'I'll be back when I hear them whistle the drawbridge up. And as for Joshua – can you not mind the boy on board?'

Hope rose in Joshua's heart, but his father hesitated.

'You being specksioneer, an' all,' said Esther, coolly.

'Aye, aye, all right.' His father relented. 'But, son, you must do what the crew tell you, and watch where you step. For a ship is a place of danger even when she's in port.'

Chapter 4

Joshua tied Nelson to a rail where he could watch him, waved Esther back over the bridge, and dropped down the cold metal ladder to the deck of his father's ship, where he sat at the foot of the mainmast, trying to take up as little room as possible. Joshua had been on his father's herring-boats often enough, and had heard all his tales of the whaling ships he had crewed years before – but to feel a real mast at his back, and solid planks underfoot was so different. About him the deck was cluttered with coils of rope, barrels, and boxes, and on every side sailors rushed fore and aft. It seemed so chaotic at first, but as he watched he saw the way order

29

was gradually imposed as the stores were sorted and stowed. Above him the masts rose taller than any tree he knew on the moor, criss-crossed by yards, booms, spars – he didn't know the right words – and hung about with ropes and rigging like the work of some monstrous sea-spider. His eye was drawn up, higher and higher, to what looked for all the world like a beer-barrel, strapped to the very top of the foremast.

'T' crow's nest,' said Thomas as he passed, laden with a bundle of long wooden poles. 'For t' look-out to spy whale spouts. Or icebergs.' Joshua stared skywards. 'It's t' one place on a ship like this where un can find a kind o' peace,' his father continued, looking up too. 'But at a price paid in shivers, son.' He stood still a moment, then tapped the bundle in his arms. 'I'm taking these harpoon staves below. Will you come?'

Joshua followed him eagerly through the forward hatch and down a steep and narrow companionway. Below decks was even busier than above, as the men worked briskly to stow the last of the stores in cramped quarters. The ceilings were low, and at times even Joshua had to duck. His father led him down to the main hold, where he lashed the bundle of staves to a bulkhead. Regiments of barrels paraded across the deck. His father kicked the nearest, which resounded with a hollow thump. 'Sounds empty, eh, son?' Joshua nodded, but his father shook his head. 'If we fill all these with whale oil and blubber we'll come back wealthy men.' He kicked it again, harder this time. 'So right now they are filled with our dreams.'

As his father lead him astern, Joshua patted another barrel. 'And mine,' he whispered. The smell of new-cut wood was fresh down here, and many of the beams had clearly been replaced in the recent work. Joshua wondered what had happened to the old ones, but didn't ask.

They moved on aft through a dark and airless passageway to a tiny cabin near the stern. There was just enough headroom for his father to stand, but not enough floor space to take more than one step in any direction. There was a bunk, a clothes locker, and a tiny desk for writing or chart-work. 'My home for the next few months, son. What do you think?'

'It's . . . small,' Joshua said. He wanted to leave something in the cabin, something to soften the bare wooden walls, something to link his father back to land. He patted his pockets and found nothing.

A whistle sounded above, followed by a booming voice. 'Make ready for sea,' the captain called.

When they emerged on deck, there were already sailors in the rigging, preparing the sails. Others manned the oars in a little group of rowing boats at the ship's bow, handing lines to the sailors on deck. Others yet were on the quayside, where they dragged heavy ropes towards the first of the capstans spaced there at at intervals.

Joshua looked about anxiously, fearing that the moment he dreaded was nigh; but his father offered a reprieve. 'It'll be slow progress what with the boats and the warping along the quay, so I reckon you can stay on board till we're past the bridge, son,' he said.

Joshua returned to his station at the mainmast foot, where, after more shouted orders and much activity about him, he finally felt the ship move. Above him Nelson strained on his leash, staring intently downwards. Joshua knew how he felt. 'I'll be back,' he said. 'Promise.'

Foot by foot the ship moved along the quay until, as they neared the bridge, a shrill whistle rang out from the bridgekeeper's hut. After a short pause the ramshackle old drawbridge which linked the two halves of the town swung upwards to allow the *Lindisfarne* through. All eyes were on her rigging, fearful lest it tangle with the split halves of the narrow bridge, close on either side. Neither Joshua, nor his father, nor anyone else on board, noticed at first the figure running to the bridge from the market on the old town side, waving as she went – but they soon heard her voice. 'Farewell, Thomas, farewell. Come home safe and come home soon.'

Suddenly she saw Joshua, waving back at her. Her tone changed in an instant. 'Joshua! No!' she shrieked. The drawbridge lowered again astern of the *Lindisfarne*, and Esther rushed across, jumping the gap before it had fully closed, to run alongside.

Joshua's father laughed as he called up at her. 'Fear not, Esther. I'm not taking him, too.' He winked at Joshua and lowered his voice. 'Not this time, anyhow.' He indicated the ladders set into the stone of the quay. 'Up any one of those son. Take care,' he said, then hugged Joshua briefly, and turned back to his work.

Joshua picked his way across the deck and stepped on to the next ladder as the ship drew past. He clambered slowly up, salt tears stinging his eyes so that he couldn't quite see the rungs, and wanting nothing more than to stay on board and set off north to sea.

Esther helped him on to the quay and wiped away his tears. She patted the knapsack he still bore on his back. 'He'll need that, Joshua. And all that's in it.' She held out a sprig of dried heather, tied together with blue ribbon. 'And here, something for his cabin.'

Joshua raced back down the ladder. His father looked at Esther, palms spread wide in question. She pointed, and mimed the carrying of a knapsack, aware that the distress of departure had hit father and son alike.

Joshua scampered below to his father's cabin, where he hung the bag on a hook, and laid the heather on the bunk. He took a big breath and one last look around, then climbed back up, to the deck and then the quay, this time with no tears.

He didn't want to speed his father's departure, but he did want to be busy, so he joined the harbourmen on the quayside capstan, pushing against a beam to turn the windlass and wind in the warp, to draw the ship onward, northward and further to sea.

As they worked and moved forward, capstan by capstan, out of the shelter of the harbour and on to the pier, he felt the tug of the wind in his hair, and heard the captain's call to unfurl the sails. There was a rippling sound above, as the sails spilled down, one after another. The ship steadily gained in speed as each sail was secured and sheeted in, so that the capstan's work grew lighter and lighter and finally was not needed at all.

The *Lindisfarne*, now free of all tethers and warps, glided past the pier with her sails billowing brilliantly. Joshua and Esther walked alongside her amid a loose gaggle of harbourmen, sweethearts and wives, all waving and shouting out and wishing her good fortune, a rich haul and, most of all, a safe journey home. The sailors on deck and in the rigging raised their caps and waved back.

The pier ended bluntly at the harbour light base, and the ship swept by. A harbourman called out, 'Three cheers for the *Lindisfarne* and her crew.' Joshua yelled himself hoarse with his hip-hip-hoorays, shouting his heart out after all that mattered most in his world, sailing away northwards and out of his life.

The crowd slowly drifed away in quiet twos and threes as the ship grew steadily smaller. Joshua lingered until he and his aunt were the last. She took his hand and led him gently away, feeling him turn every few steps to look seawards at the receding ship.

He said nothing, not even when they collected a frantic Nelson from his post, guarding a now-empty berth. He remained silent as they passed through the old town and climbed up the steep hill above it. As they emerged beside the abbey, the seascape opened behind them, and Joshua turned one last time. A flag snapped on the tower of St Mary's Church below them, just beneath a weather vane in the shape of a ship. Joshua watched it swing in the wind, and saw behind it, some three leagues distant, the flash of some new white sails, right next to the great bronze N.

Chapter 5

For days after his father had gone, Joshua spoke not a word, not even to Nelson. He went about his daily tasks dutifully enough but it seemed to Esther that he was somewhere else entirely, whatever the work at hand.

And he was. When he raked the cottage fires he was scrubbing the *Lindisfarne*'s deck. When fetching firewood he was bringing up food from her stores. When he tended the cows or the sheep he was watching the wind in her sails, sheeting in here, letting out there, adjustments to keep her moving sweetly onwards, even if northwards and further away.

And when, exhausted, he climbed into his

hammock, which he had re-slung to face north, it was in his father's cabin he swung, clutching a sprig of heather in one hand and the key to his father's chest in the other.

His first words were directed at a cow as she lurched downhill, away from the herd, on the way in for milking. 'Luff up there, Mustard, and come to port,' he shouted after the lumbering beast. The sound of his own voice surprised him, and astonished Nelson, but the cow understood nautical orders no better than it did his more familiar landlubber coaxing.

'That's not Mustard,' said a bright young voice at the farmyard gate. Joshua turned to see Emmy, his cousin, standing with the sunset behind her, gilding her red hair. '*That's* Mustard.' She pointed at another, more obedient cow, in the midst of the small herd.

'She's always been Mustard to me,' said Joshua, smiling down at her as she swung the gate open for him and the herd.

'That doesn't mean she *is* Mustard,' Emmy insisted.

'Then what name do you give her?'

Emmy shrugged. 'Not-Mustard. Cress. It doesn't matter.' She closed the gate. 'Cows don't answer to names anyway.'

Joshua paused a moment, while the cows

stood about, uncertainly. 'No,' he said, 'I don't suppose they do.' He ushered the animals into the milking shed. Emmy followed and helped get them into their stalls. With work to do she fell quiet again, until the cows were all in place, and Joshua had set to with the milking.

She stood beside his milking stool, stroking the cow's side in time with the the jets of milk splashing into the pail. 'I like it that you're speaking again, Joshua,' she said. 'So will Ma.'

'Is she not at market?'

Emmy shook her head. 'Pa's gone today.'

There was a pause in the rhythm of the milk-spray. Emmy knew what Joshua was thinking. Whenever her father went to market he called at all the inns on the way back, where he drank away most of his profit, before he rolled noisily home, looking for someone to vent his anger on. It was usually Joshua.

'It's all right,' said Emmy. 'He's taken Laurence.'

Joshua nodded. With Emmy's elder brother in tow there'd be no drink tonight for Flint, and maybe, at last, a chance at the chest. 'Just you and me and your ma at table, then?' he asked, trying not to sound too hopeful.

'That's right,' said Emmy. 'And I'd better go and help.' She scampered into the kitchen, while Joshua returned to his milking.

'Give me some of your patience, Mustard,' he said, as he rested his forehead on her warm flank. 'I'm going to need it.'

The milking was the last of Joshua's jobs that day, and he was soon chasing away his chill before the fire, while Emmy and her mother set the table. Normally he'd enjoy a supper with Flint and Laurence gone, but tonight, welcome though the food was, he could not wait for the meal to be over, and grew ever more conscious of the key hanging heavy about his neck. It seemed an age before Emmy's second yawn signalled her bedtime. The moment her mother took her upstairs to the tiny attic bedroom, Joshua bounded across to the darkened corner of the room.

He slid the cushions off the dark wooden lid of the chest, and undid his shirt so he could loop the key over his head. He was so jittery at first he couldn't get the key to fit, but then the heavy tumblers of the lock yielded, and with two quick turns the clasp was undone.

All he saw when he raised the lid were old sea boots and much-patched fishing sweaters. As he moved them aside something glittered below, and on reaching in his hand touched chill metal. Joshua pulled out a brass hand compass, half-spilled out from its stiff leather pouch. It was tarnished and scratched, but the needle still swung freely. Joshua watched its arc grow smaller, until he realised it was pointing directly at him. He quickly turned the compass over, and saw an inscription on the back of the case, which he couldn't make out in the flickering firelight.

A timber creaked overhead and Joshua froze, listening hard. He had heard the noises the stairs made often enough to know that she wasn't coming down, at least not yet. He replaced the compass and rummaged in the second layer of clothes. A thick flannel shirt seemed to be wrapped around something. Joshua pulled it out and unfolded the arms to find an oval pewter picture frame, about the size of his hand. He held it up for a better look. Beneath broken glass a young woman stared out at him through steady eyes. Dark curls pushed out from under her bonnet, framing brightly glowing cheeks and a sad smile. Joshua sat for a long time with the picture on his lap, oblivious to everything around him.

'She was pretty wasn't she?' Soft though it was, Esther's voice behind startled him, and he scrambled to repack the chest, until her hand on his shoulder told him it was all right, and he could relax.

'I don't remember her,' he said flatly. It wasn't

entirely true, for there were things he did remember – her voice singing him to sleep, the smell of her hair, the touch of her hand on his brow – even if he couldn't pull them together into a complete picture, like the one he held in his hands.

'What happened?' he ventured, knowing he could never ask his father.

His aunt waited a long time before she replied. 'She was ill, even then. See the colour in her cheeks? It seemed to go on for years, but no one was really sure when it started. You came early into the world, and caught her out of doors in a bitter north wind, but she always said it wasn't that. Your father was at sea, tossed by the same gale. He came home and there you were: he'd not hear a word said against north winds after that.' The fire crackled, shooting sparks on to the hearth.

'She seemed fine while she nursed you, then grew slowly weaker. Your father worked hisself to the bone, paying doctors and apothecaries. Then he stayed ashore to care for her, and for you, but he carried on paying, till all they had left was debt. It was no use, in the end.' She looked up at a noise outside the window, then down at him. 'Such dedication is rare in a man.'

Now Joshua too heard Flint's familiar

growling voice on the path, and they both stood up. 'Lock it away, Joshua,' Esther said, as she went to the door. 'I won't tell.' Joshua hurriedly packed the chest, not quite sure whether her cheerful chatter with husband and son in the kitchen was intended to give him time, or whether she meant it. Later, in his hammock, he decided it must have been both.

When school resumed after Easter there was a new teacher in charge. Joshua and his classmates, Laurence among them, watched warily as he settled himself into his chair, casting his eye about, like a general sizing up an army ranged against him. Joshua didn't like the look of him at all, outnumbered though he was.

His voice, when it came, rasped roughly round the silent classroom. 'My name is Hestall. *Mister* Hestall. You will call me sir.' None of them dared to catch his eye. 'And now you will tell me *your* names.'

He prowled past the desks, with the register held before him, while each terrified child called out his name before being permitted to sit. Joshua could see Laurence tremble in front of him as his turn approached. 'Laurence Flint,' he piped feebly.

Joshua closed his eyes, but couldn't help

hearing the thwack as Hestall clipped Laurence across the head. 'Moments ago, boy, I told you to call me sir,' he roared. 'Is your memory so short?'

Laurence blustered desperately. 'Yes, sir. No, sir. Laurence Flint, sir!' Hestall thrust him down into his seat and moved on to Joshua.

'Joshua Murphy, sir,' he sang out, as calmly and clearly as he could. Hestall seemed satisfied till he checked the register, which he slammed shut under Joshua's nose. 'I have you here as Flint,' he hissed, with snake-narrow eyes.

Joshua looked straight ahead. 'I'm Joshua Murphy.' He blinked. 'Sir.'

'You DARE to contradict me, boy?' Joshua found himself dragged by the ear to the front of the room, then spun round to face the class. Hestall had found what he wanted: an example. 'I have served in Her Majesty's army and I will not – I WILL NOT – brook insolence from a snivelling boy!' He seemed even angrier when he saw that Joshua was not snivelling at all, and paced furiously round the room till he spotted the globe by the window. He kicked Joshua towards it, and set it spinning.

'I have travelled the world, boy. I have been to every corner of our glorious Empire.' He spun the globe faster and faster, till the multiple colours of the land and the blue of the ocean merged into a blur. Only the patches of white at the top and bottom stayed constant. Hestall looked slowly round the class. 'Today's lesson is geography, and I will beat you, Joshua Flint, for each mistake you or your class-mates make.'

His pudgy hand slammed down on the north pole and the globe stopped abruptly. A finger jabbed at a patch of pink. 'Where, boy, is this?' he yelled. Joshua paused to prepare for the blow before he admitted he didn't know, but the force of it still took him by surprise.

The globe spun again, and, as a way out of his torture, Joshua concentrated all his thought on the white spaces near the top and the deep blue between. He ran through the names engraved on his heart by his father's fireside tales. Greenland. Baffin Bay. Iceland. The Denmark Straight. He tried to guess where the *Lindisfarne* was now. 'WELL?' screamed Hestall, obliterating Orkney with a shower of spit. Orkney. The whalers put in there to provision and complete their crew. Perhaps there'd be a letter soon.

Joshua followed Hestall's prodding finger, prepared for more blows but relieved that he knew this one. 'Newfoundland, sir,' he said firmly.

The unexpected thump in his side winded him

badly. 'Rubbish, boy! It's Canada, another of our Queen's Dominions!'

Joshua knew he was right, and had met Newfoundlander mates of his father, but held his peace throughout the beating till Hestall tired of his sport and hurled him back to his desk. 'Because of this boy's ignorance,' Hestall wheezed, 'this entire class will stay behind today until you *all* learn just how far our Empire spreads.'

Joshua stared ahead. His limbs were numb, his head was ringing, and the pain washed up in waves. He saw, through his dizziness, the scowls from the children about him, especially Laurence: but he was undaunted. He knew who he was, and he knew what he knew, and that could never be beaten out of him, not by an entire regiment of Hestalls.

Chapter 6

Emmy liked school – no Hestall for her – but always looked forward to the end of the last class. She'd be the first out of the door, bounding across the playground to the grass bank opposite, where waited Nelson. He was always pleased to see her, and she'd sit and stroke his ears till the older class finished. She did not really mind that his tail wagged warmer then for Joshua than it ever did for her. She enjoyed the walk home along between-field paths, even if Joshua had been quieter still just lately.

But today the bank was empty. She looked about and whistled, but knew there was no point, for Nelson told the time as well as any watch. If he was going to be there he'd be there by now. She waited, with an anxious frown, till Laurence and his class-mates spilled out of the schoolroom. Joshua was not among them. She listened for the shouting that would say Hestall had kept him back again, but the classroom was quiet.

'Where is he?' she asked as Laurence dawdled up.

'Who?' he shrugged. 'Dog or dog-boy?'

Emmy stood up. 'Joshua, of course. He came with us this morning.'

'Well he wasn't here this afternoon. Lucky devil.' Laurence set off along the narrow road. 'I'd skulk off too, but Father'd beat me worse than Hestall does if ever he found out.'

'Won't he beat Joshua?'

'Not if you don't tell him. Hestall's easier on us if Joshua's not around, and that's the way I'd like to keep it.'

They walked on a way in silence. Emmy pondered what it was about Joshua that fired Hestall's anger so. She had heard, again and again, the yelling through the classroom wall, so loud at times it made the tiny ones about her cry. 'I wonder where he is?' she said, more to herself than to Laurence.

He shrugged. 'Don't know. Don't really care. But he and t' dog will be together. Find one and you'll find t' other.'

Laurence was right. Nelson and Joshua sat side by side atop Beacon Hill, staring northwards out to sea. Though it was far too soon to expect the whalers back, Joshua scanned the horizon for ships, while Nelson, who did not know what he was supposed to be looking for, waited for rabbits to pop out of the thicket below him. Beyond the thicket the grassy slope dropped steeply away to the cliff edge, where the lighthouse stood, squat and freshly whitewashed. They were level with the weather vane on its top, showing the wind to be northerly, driving an onshore swell.

Far below, the sails on the fishing cobles swung back and forth like russet pendulums as the swell rolled by beneath them. The tide was low but rising, and away to the west the waves broke foamy upon the scattered knuckles of Whitby Rock. A two-masted ship stood away seawards, biding her time till the tide rose high enough to allow her over the bar and into the harbour. With the onshore wind and the swell surging between the entrance piers, the approach would be a tricky one; and though he knew neither vessel nor crew, Joshua felt for them, delayed as they were in their homecoming, by tide and wind and wave.

He wanted to wait until the ship was safely past the piers, but Nelson's gathering restlessness told him it was school-out time, and he realised with a start he'd better head home. He had to be sure Laurence wasn't there first to give him away. It wasn't as if Flint wanted an education for him, but if he learnt Joshua was neither at his books, as an example to Laurence, nor behind the plough in the field, there'd be another beating for sure.

Joshua stood up. 'Aye, Nelson,' he said. 'Time to go.'

They set off to the farm, anxiety rising within Joshua like the tide far below. He kept looking across the fields, until he spotted two small figures approaching the farm from the other direction. He vaulted the gate, startling the cows in the meadow, and sprinted over the springy turf, suppressing the desire to shout after his cousins in case Flint was about. He ran ahead of them, waving furiously, but couldn't attract their attention, so when the hedge next thinned out he plunged through it, and tumbled into the lane below. He lay breathless, mud-spattered, with clothing snagged and hedgerow in his hair. A thorn had scratched his cheek.

'Well, well,' sneered Laurence, who'd recovered from his surprise faster then Emmy. 'Our hedgehog friend. A proper little urchin.'

'Hey-up, Pirate,' said Emmy, as Nelson broke off from seeing Joshua safe to wag his way up to her. He ignored Laurence completely.

Joshua slowly got to his feet and dusted himself off. He decided to ignore Laurence too, at least for the moment. 'Why do you call him that?' he asked Emmy.

'Same reason you call him Nelson.' Joshua frowned. 'Because of his eye-patch. And when he and thee come crashin' through hedgerow to tumble at my feet I reckon Pirate fits him well.' She reached up to touch his graze.

Joshua winced. 'You won't tell?' he asked her.

Emmy and Laurence looked at each other and then both looked back at him. Emmy knew she should let Laurence speak.

He waited just long enough to have Joshua fretting, then spoke his verdict like a judge. 'Nay. We'll not tell. But you are beholden to us now. Dunnot forget it.'

Laurence led Emmy ahead. She looked over her shoulder at Joshua, shaking her head to show he wasn't beholden to her, but he was so intent on picking the thorns from his smock that she wasn't sure he'd seen her. And if he had, maybe he'd not understood. Her mother shook her head at him all the time, with a different meaning.

Chapter 7

For the rest of the term, as the days lengthened and the noonday sun climbed higher, Joshua only went to school when driven there by bad weather. When he did venture in Hestall beat him mercilessly: for his truancy, for being behind with his books, for the rebellion he heard in his silence; but mainly just for the sake of it. Emmy came to dread rainy days, for she knew she'd hear through wincing walls Hestall's rages, and even the thuds of his blows: and it was almost worse because there was never a sound from Joshua. Even Laurence came to feel sorry for him then: but any pity was tempered by envy at his freedom whenever the rain didn't come.

Joshua lived for the days when he could sit amongst the wind-carved gorse bushes on the brow of Beacon Hill, and survey the sea below him as if it were his kingdom, and this hilltop den his throne. Faithful Nelson crouched alongside him like an eager earl, eyeing the white-capped waves as if he could shepherd them home. Joshua whiled away his many hours there by twisting the gorse branches to form a kind of bower against the wind, which he patched with strips of canvas to keep away the rain. He laid a floor of twigs and leaves, and carpeted it with sackcloth scraps and stolen handfuls of straw. By half-term his shelter was so sound that he needn't go to school at all. Instead he sat, listening to the patter of rain on his roof, and drinking in the exotic coconut smell of the gorse flowers around him. He knew of the South Sea islanders Captain Cook had encountered, living in palm-fronded huts amid fragrant flowers, when he travelled the world in his tough little Whitby ships. But Joshua's thoughts never lingered long in these regions, before they were directed north, like migrating geese, to chilly arctic waters, where the only flowers were made of ice, and only ships gave shelter. And the time when those ships were due home was drawing closer: another month, maybe. Two at the most.

When the school term was over, and the long summer break began, he could no longer fool Flint that he was in class, and was put to work in the fields. Any time he spent in his hilltop refuge was limited to stolen evening hours. Each night he watched the shadows lengthen and the blue-grey haze of twilight settle like smoke, until the lighthouse keeper lit his lantern, and his beam began its familiar sweep. On the darkening waters below fishing-boat lamps flickered in answer, telling Joshua it was time to go home, where even Emmy had given up asking where he had been. Each time he left the den for his farmhouse hammock, he carved another notch in the gnarled trunk of the nearest gorse bush, to join the many notches already there – one for every day his father had been gone. There wasn't much space left for more, but Joshua never considered he might need another trunk. Any day now, he thought. Maybe tomorrow.

One Thursday morning he was labouring in the upper meadow, lost in thought, when he was roused by Emmy's shouting. 'A sail, Joshy, look! They're coming in!' she piped as she ran from the hedgerow, where she had been picking poppies with her mother.

Joshua leapt to his feet and dashed to the cliff edge, desperately hoping she was right, and berating himself for not seeing them first. He'd waited for this moment so intently, and for so long, it didn't seem right that it should fall to anyone else. But as it was Emmy he forgave her. He stared in the direction of her outstretched arm, and saw, arrayed against the horizon, the unmistakable outline of three Whitby whalers, heading home in the autumn sun. His hope soared so high he could not stand still but paced back and forth on the cliff edge, never taking his eye off the approaching vessels.

'Watch your footing, Joshua,' called his aunt. He glanced down, and jumped backwards when he saw how close he was to the cliff edge, nibbled and gnawed as it was by hungry winter storms. He looked up at her, with pleading eyes. She smiled back. 'No more work today. We'll go to town and meet them come in.'

The three of them were soon bustling along the cliff path towards town. Joshua ran on ahead from one vantage point to the next, and so intent on the ever-nearer ships that he tripped over twice. But his outward excitement hid a vague disquiet that had seeded inside him soon after the ships were sighted, and now grew stronger with every wave that broke against their bows.

The Whitby whaling fleet was nine strong that year, and the incoming vessels were the first three home. Joshua had never before considered the possibility that his father's ship would not be first back, but now it dawned cruelly upon him. He had only seen her briefly, but he knew the *Lindisfarne*'s lines as well as the shape of his shoes, and could pick her out from any fleet as a lamb does its mother from the flock. And he knew, in his now-leaden heart, that none of the ships coming in were his father's.

As they passed the abbey his aunt at last allowed him to run on ahead. He hurtled down to Church Street and across the bridge to join the people gathering on the west pier. He weaved his way through the happy crowd to the end of the pier, where he stepped up on to the rampart of the huge sea wall. Immediately his fears were realised. He waited until the ships were close enough to read their names – *Esk, Henrietta, Volunteer* – then turned away, trying not to see the excited faces and waving arms of the crowd behind him. He stepped down on to the pier, his hopes sinking like stones, and walked slowly back to the bridge just as Aunt Esther and Emmy approached. Both knew immediately from his face what he'd learnt. Esther laid her hand on his shoulder, and drew him to the edge as the first ship passed below. They peered down at the sailors busy on deck, gap-toothed grins on their weather-beaten faces. 'Any word of the *Lindisfarne*?' Esther called.

The bosun looked up, squinting in the sun. 'No, ma'am. Not since before Mayday, when there were scarcely a whale. She and t' *Phantom* struck north for richer pickings, and no word from either since. I dursay she'll not be long behind us.'

Joshua heard this too, but was too overwhelmed by disappointment to take comfort from it, at least until later, as he sat in his den. Nelson sensed a need to crouch closer, and Joshua reached out to stroke his velvety ears. 'You know how to wait, eh, boy? All those times outside the classroom, you were always there. I'll bet you thought every boy who came out was me, eh?' Nelson yawned. 'But did you never wonder – *what if he doesn't come*?'

Nelson licked his wrist, as if to say he was never troubled by such doubts, while Joshua talked on. 'I always thought t' *Lindisfarne* would be first back. Don't know what made me so sure. But if she's not first, second, or third . . . she might not even be last. What then, boy? You and me and Flint?' Joshua shivered, despite the warmth of the sun. 'What then?' Joshua fell silent, and sat so still, for so many hours, that when darkness fell and Nelson took him home he was stiff-legged and limping like an old old man.

The same cruel sequence – sails spotted, soaring hopes, bitter disappointment – was repeated three times in the next two weeks, and each time the hope was more desperate and the disappointment more crushing. Then the ships stopped coming in at all. No *Lindisfarne*. No *Phantom*. No word. Nothing.

Chapter 8

The day after the harvest festival, Esther served autumn's first breakfast of porridge. Joshua sat at the table, enthusiastically spooning it up, with Emmy and Laurence beside him. He finished before them and slipped down to get his coat and bag.

'And where are you going?' growled Flint from his deep chair by the fire.

'Why, to school.' Joshua was getting good at lying, at least to Flint, and looked forward to his first full day back at the den now the summer break was over.

'Oh no you're not.' A match rasped and flared beneath his whiskered chin as he lit his pipe.

Joshua grew worried. Had his den been discovered? Had Laurence betrayed him? He glanced at the table, where Laurence still sat, supping his tea and looking levelly back.

'You'll work in the fields, boy, to pay for your porridge.'

'But Father's paid you already.'

There was a pause. The air around Flint was heavy with pipe smoke and menace. 'Oh? And where'd you hear that? A-snooping round my hearth?'

Joshua fell silent: he knew protest, at least from him, was useless, but he was surprised when Aunt Esther spoke up: 'Frank, the lad needs schooling too.'

Flint stood up. 'It's plain enough his father's frozen in and won't be back this winter, whatever he promised. So he'll not bide here in my house without he works his keep.'

Esther stood very still. 'It's *our* house, Frank. And do not forget 'tis my brother you speak of so.'

Flint brought his fist down on the mantelpiece and roared. 'Enough, woman! My mind's made up. There's stubble in Ten-Acre Top needs firing and I'll expect it done when I'm back from market.' He stomped off, and let the heavy kitchen door slam shut behind him.

No one had put it into words before Flint, though all knew it to be true: if the *Lindisfarne* wasn't back by now she must be frozen fast, and forced to winter in the ice till next spring's thaw. A whole year he would have to wait. It would be a long cold time, for both father and son. Joshua looked at Esther, then put down his bag and picked up his boots. 'It's all right,' he said. 'I like outdoors.'

It was only later, when she took him a lunch of bread, cheese and apple, that Esther saw any sign of feeling in his face, and even then she couldn't be sure, because he was standing to leeward of the stubble-smoke as she approached, and it was dense enough to make anyone's eyes water.

'Here, Joshua,' she said, as she laid her muslin-wrapped bundle on the grass at the edge of the field, and sat beside it. 'A bite o' lunch.' He nodded his thanks and sat down too. He wiped his brow, smudging the soot marks across his face. She smiled at the sight. 'You look like a miner,' she said.

He frowned, then guessed what his face must look like when he saw his soot-blackened hands. He waved them at the water and smiled back. 'A mariner is all I ever want to be, Aunt Esther.'

'Aye, I know,' she replied, quietly. 'Though

Lord knows they're both dangerous enough trades.' She surveyed the smouldering soil as they ate. 'You've worked hard, Joshua. How much more?' He pointed to what remained, his mouth full of food.

'Well I'm taking these eggs to Mother Crowley, and I'll fetch Emmy and Laurence after. Will you be done by then?'

Joshua shook his head, and pretended to eat on. 'Don't think so,' he said eventually, though he knew he could be if he wanted to. An empty farmhouse was too good an opportunity to miss and there was something in it he had to have, especially now.

The weather worsened daily as autumn wore on into winter. His father's too-big jerseys kept out the worst of the wind as Joshua laboured in the fields, but grew heavy and chilling in rain. Even then, when darkness fell and Esther called him in he took his warming broth without a word of complaint.

'Are you not frozen?' she'd ask. 'It's bitter out.'

He'd look at her and rub red hands together before the fire. ''Tis colder yet where Father is,' he said once. After that he just shook his head and hid his shivers.

At night he'd swing in his hammock and listen. The chimneys past which the wind whistled were the mast-stumps of a winter-rigged ship. Cows lowing in the byre outside were polar bears, hungry and curious and wanting in. And when coals settled in the grate below, they were ship's timbers cracking as the pack-ice closed its vice-like grip.

One night he woke long before dawn to unaccustomed silence. There was no wind at all, the beasts were quiet, and the fire was nothing but ashes. Clouds of vapour hung over him as he breathed, and misted the window over. He stretched across to it and rubbed a porthole clear. The landscape outside was transformed by a thick white carpet of snow, ensilvered by moonlight.

Joshua grinned. Snow came rarely to Whitby, but here it was, in arctic volumes. He swung silently down, and quickly donned as many layers of clothing as he could find. He roused Nelson gently, slipped the latch, and stepped outside to gasp at the beauty all around him. So this is what it was like.

As soon as he had cleared the farmyard he stopped, ankle deep in the powdery whiteness, and craned his neck backwards. Overhead the stars glittered brilliantly against the sky, like diamonds on a black velvet dress. He picked out the ones his father had named for him. There was Orion, the hunter, and at his heel his dog, Sirius: but where his father had shown him a sword, hanging from the hunter's belt, Joshua now saw a harpoon. Joshua pointed out Sirius to Nelson, who snuffled drowsily at his feet. 'That's your star, boy,' he whispered, puffing great clouds of breath, but Nelson paid it no heed and huddled closer for warmth.

Joshua turned to find the Plough, and traced the guide stars upwards from its blade to Polaris, the North Star, the axis of the heavens. Somewhere far from here, but closer to the north pole and its marking star, the same constellations hung in the sky above his father's head, and similar snow encased his feet. Joshua stared until his neck hurt. He had promised to wait, and to hope. What else could he do?

When he dropped his gaze at last, he saw the long shadows cast by the low half-moon. Between them lay a sparkling path, which pulled him northwards over the snow. As he stepped crunchily forward, Nelson's sleepiness and puzzlement fell away, and he scampered ahead with excited but snow-muffled yelps, till Joshua called him to heel.

Without knowing why, Joshua wanted to visit

his den. What with the cold and the dark and the work, he hadn't been for some time now, and tonight it felt right. He couldn't help smiling at the polar landscape around him, comforted to know he shared something with his father. Once they were over the ridge from the farmhouse, he laughed outright at Nelson's reactions to snowballs – but only briefly, for when he topped Beacon Hill, he saw the wreckage of his refuge. His gorse bush bower was torn apart. The bushes themselves were uprooted, and his straw floor and sack-cloth roof scattered widely about, like lambswool after a fox had been by. He stood on the brow of the hill, taking in the devastation while behind him lighthouse sweeps answered the moon. This was the work of no storm.

He traced his footprints back, not smiling now, as the lightening eastern horizon heralded the sun. It *had* to be Laurence. He approached the farmhouse and noted the curl of woodsmoke from its chimney. A figure, dark-shrouded against the snow, huddled forwards: Aunt Esther. 'Is it not enough to disappear by day that you have to go roaming by night now too?' she pleaded. 'And on such a night as this?' She took his frozen hand and led him home.

I'll wander no more, Aunt Esther. I've nowhere to go, he thought. He really didn't know whether he'd said it aloud.

Over breakfast, as he thawed, Joshua listened to Flint's grumbles, and tried to guess what work lay ahead, for even on a Sunday there was no rest for him. But it was Esther's voice he heard the clearest, ringing out like a winter bell. 'No, Frank,' she said. 'Not in this snow, and not today. 'Tis the Sabbath, and I'll take him to town, for midwinter service at St Mary's. Emmy and Laurence will join us. You may come or stay, as you please.'

'There'll be no cart in this weather,' Flint objected.

'Then we'll walk.' The firmness in her voice averted further protest.

And walk they did. Emmy squealed with delight when she stepped outside but Laurence didn't like the cold. The snowballs he flung at Joshua were studded with stones, and hurled with a venom he never let his mother witness.

St Mary's was very different from the village church near the school where Joshua usually went. It stood below the abbey ruins on the very brow of the hill above the harbour, looking more out to sea than down to the town where its parishioners lived. The path to the door was lined by tombstones, much weathered away, but Joshua could make out, here and there, anchors and nets and the unmistakable shape of a boat. His eye was drawn against his will to the inscriptions, but when it ran across the words '. . . lost in the Greenland seas . . .' Joshua could read no more, and his gaze snapped upwards to the sundial over the door. It cast no shadow today.

Within, the church was busy, and Esther ushered them to a cramped pew below the huge three-decker pulpit. There was much about the building to call to mind a ship – stout wooden beams and pillars, fine panelling, and gleaming brass lamps and ornaments – but the people filing in were little like a crew. Joshua stared at the ladies and gentlemen in their town finery as they slipped into their private family pews. He watched how they glanced slyly about, but only ever saw their own kind. Not one of them noticed him, but he took in all the details of their clothes, right down to the sound the silk made when the ladies sat down.

The service was long and dull, and Joshua soon stopped listening. He looked around at the building and its ornaments, intrigued at the ear trumpet especially installed for the vicar's deaf wife. She held it to her ear when he preached his sermon from above, but even her eyes glazed over towards the end. Behind her memorial stones lined the wall, with names and dates and coats of arms. There was something familiar about one of them. He leant closer to peer at it, till Esther nudged him sharply, and the congregation stood.

'And our final hymn is for those in peril on the sea, especially our Whitby ships beset in the polar ice. Number 453: From Greenland's Icy Mountains.'

Next to him Laurence fumbled through the hymn book to find the place, but Joshua had no need, for he knew this one by heart, and could look about while he sang. As the service had dragged on and the light outside grown dimmer, the oil lamps scattered round the church shone ever more brightly, raising reflections in the richly polished wood of pew and pulpit. His father had told him that all the oil in all the lamps of the land came from whales caught by him and his fellow whalers far afield. Now it seemed as if the missing men were here in spirit, bringing light in the darkness of winter to their townsfolk and colleagues, and kin.

As he sang, his hand slipped inside his jersey to the leather case that had hung round his neck, day and night, since Flint had said his father wasn't coming back. He slid the heavy compass into his hand, and felt the metal chill against his skin. His fingers rubbed the casing, and when he felt the raised edges of the inscription his singing suddenly stopped. He looked up at the familiar stone on the wall again, but didn't need to peer at it now, for he knew what the motto there said, if not what it meant. The same strange words were inscribed into his father's compass, now safely cradled in his hand: *Spero meliora*.

Filing out of the church, behind the gentry, Joshua lingered by the memorial stone, seeking a clue to the meaning of the motto, but found none.

'Better things,' boomed the vicar's voice behind him.

'Sir?' queried Joshua.

'*Spero meliora*, my boy. The Scoresby family motto. Latin, don't y'know.' He had already turned away to the vestry, as if unaware of Joshua's urgent need for understanding: but at the door he looked back, and relented. 'It means *I hope for better things*.' He opened the door and slipped inside, muttering as he went, 'Don't we all, boy, don't we all.'

Chapter 9

The companionship of Nelson, secret kindnesses from Esther and Emmy, and a still-fresh hope for better things, were all Joshua had to sustain him through a long winter of bullying and back-breaking work. He no longer counted the days, for he knew there would be so many: he simply endured, and waited, knowing that his father and his crewmates must do the same, while they served out their sentence in their icy prison, before the promised freedom of spring.

By Easter the equinoctial gales had almost blown out, but the kitchen windows still rattled when Joshua sat down to his meagre supper, flanked by his cousins. He watched Esther depart for the scullery but failed to watch his plate. Laurence, emboldened by Flint's absence at market, shot his arm across, like a striking viper, to snap up the last paltry morsels of meat. He held them to his open mouth, then offered them to Joshua, before snatching his hand away at the last moment. His weasel eyes narrowed as he enjoyed the torment written on Joshua's face. He looked across at Emmy. 'Who shall have this?' he asked, as the bacon shuttled back and forth, never quite reaching Joshua's hands or his own lips, at least until Esther returned, when it vanished behind his cruel grinning teeth.

Afterwards, in his hammock, Joshua laid the compass on his stomach, in the hope that its cool weight might ease the hunger pains which kept him awake. He heard the crashing door, the stomping boots and the gruff growl which announced Flint's return. The drunker he got the louder he spoke, and tonight it was as if there was no wall to muffle him.

All these were familiar sounds, but then came something new: the rattle of a padlock, a frustrated roar, and then the thump of heavy boots on wood. 'Frank!' pleaded Esther. 'Stop it!'

'Where's the key, woman?' he roared. He could only be talking about the chest.

'I don't know.' There was a new note of fear in Esther's voice.

'Did he not leave it with you? His dear sister?' Another kick. 'Then it must be with the boy.' Heavy steps toward the scullery door.

Esther's steps were quicker, and when she spoke, the way her voice made the door ring told how hard she was pressed up against it, as she barred Flint's path. 'Why now, Frank? He's sleeping.'

'Why now? Because his father's not coming back, that's why now.' Joshua heard, but could not take in what he had said. He lay perfectly still.

'There's a frigate in Hartlepool dock, just come down from Orkney. Word has come down with her. T'*Phantom* is free of the ice and limping in. But t'*Lindisfarne*'s not with her, nor is she expected back. Some terrible storm.'

Esther's voice was different now: flat and cold and numb. 'Is it certain?'

'Aye, as certain as the fact that this is a farm, not an orphanage.' He was shouting again. 'Six long years yon boy has sheltered under my roof, and all because his father was your kin.' Joshua winced at that *was*. 'Now let me pass, for I will have that key. Yon chest and everything in it are now my own, and, if nothing else, his

Scoresby compass holds some value.'

'No, Frank! If what you say is true, then poor Thomas' scant chattels belong to Joshua, or to me. Either way you shall not pass.'

There was a loud thump, then a scream. Something heavy slammed into the scullery door and slid to the ground. The sound of sobbing drifted under the doorsill. This aside, the silence was ominous.

Joshua had felt Flint's fist often enough, and seen him lash out at Laurence on occasion: but he had never known him hit his wife. He feared what might follow, but was astonished when, instead of further blows, there were soothing sounds. It seemed that even Flint had limits, and he knew he had just overstepped them. Joshua listened as he lifted Esther whimpering to her feet, muttering softly, then half-helped, half-dragged her across the kitchen and up the stairs.

Joshua listened a long time after, hardly breathing, his gaze fixed on the ceiling beams above him. Whatever the truth of what Flint had heard, he clearly believed it, and was now bent on selling all his father's things, just as had been predicted. He clutched the compass – Thomas Murphy's Scoresby compass – closer. Whatever its value in money to Flint, it meant infinitely more to his father, and now to Joshua. He was suddenly sure of one thing, and sat up sharply at the realisation of it. Flint would never see the compass, or him, again.

He swung himself down and quickly dressed. He unhooked his bag from the door, and hurriedly packed what few possessions lay nearby. It seemed so little. Fingering the key on its cord, he paused, then gingerly opened the kitchen door and crept inside. He opened the chest and rummaged through the clothes for the sea boots and the best jumper. The trousers were too big. His mother's photograph stared up at him from the jumble within, scarcely seen in the dim red light cast by the the embers. He didn't like to close the lid on her, but he had to make the chest look as Flint had left it, to give himself more time. He shut and locked the chest, then looked around the room as if to fix in his memory what it was he was leaving.

Nelson whimpered in the scullery; he didn't like being left alone at night. Joshua knew he couldn't take him along, but if he opened the door to shush his rising whine, his resolve to leave might melt away altogether. He had to do something, for drunk though Flint was, a bark would soon rouse him to further fury. Joshua was lifting the latch to the scullery door when a whisper from the stairwell halted him.

'It's all right,' said Emmy, crouching in the shadows, where she'd been watching throughout. 'I'll quiet him.' There were tears in her eyes, when she leant forward into the firelight.

'I'm going north,' he whispered back, as he shouldered his bags.

'I know,' she said softly.

'I can't stay here, just waiting, any longer. Not now.'

'I know.' She shook her head, as if surprised he hadn't left earlier.

'I have to *do* something to find my father.'

'It's all right, Joshy. I won't tell, and I'll look after Nelson for you.'

He set down his bags and hugged her, worried at the way her skinny shoulders shivered under her nightgown. 'Thank you, Emmy,' was all he could find to say; and when she made him promise to be careful, as he had his father a year before, all he could do was nod. He wiped away a tear that slid down her cheek, and another of his own, then took up his bags once more, blew her a kiss from each of his hands, and left.

His route to the cliff path was so familiar from his months of work and wandering that it didn't matter there was no moon to guide him across the fields. Dozing cattle paid him no heed as he slipped by. 'Farewell, Not-Mustard,' he whispered to every cow he passed, and even to Mustard herself. An owl hooted in the wood as he reached the path and turned left for the town. Without breaking his stride, or even glancing back, he slipped the key-string over his head and flung it over the cliff, to the surf booming far below.

As he passed the abbey ruins, more felt than seen in the darkness, and neared the churchyard, his fear of discovery grew. He wasn't sure of the time, but he thought it possible there were still roisterers spilling out of the inns. He didn't know what they'd make of a runaway boy if they saw him.

He crouched to rest in the lee of the graveyard wall, thinking fast. There'd be no one in the church, but the steps which dropped to the town were lit by a beacon to guide the fishing boats in twixt the piers. He crept along the foot of the wall to the Donkey Road, a steep and winding alley of darkness, and set off down it.

Halfway down, a shadow, made of a thicker blackness, crossed his path, and he stopped, frozen in fear, till the purring pressure on his shins identified it as a cat. He stooped to stroke the beast, while thinking of Nelson and where to go next. A breeze wafted up, bearing the sweet smell of wood-smoke from the kipper-curing sheds, and the whinny of a horse on Church Street.

Joshua bundled up his pack as tight as it could go, and lashed the sea boots to the outside, then clasped it close to his chest, and set off at a run. There were two inns at the foot of the Donkey Road, and although lights flickered within there was no one abroad in the street. He turned into Church Street, and scampered from shadow to shadow toward the marketplace. There were passageways off to the left, and he stopped for a moment in each till he found the one he wanted. It led under an archway into a long narrow yard. Lights still burned, and voices rumbled in the coaching house to the right, while ahead stood the mail coach, glistening and sinister in the damp dark. Joshua shuddered.

There were stable doors to the left. The first was empty, but the second held a horse and a healthy flooring of straw. The animal was almost as nervous as he was, but Joshua summoned all his hard-earned husbandry skills to soothe it, first by words, and then, when it allowed, with a steady stroke on its nose. When he was sure he had gained its confidence he opened the door, slipped inside, and bolted it shut behind him.

This was a well cared-for horse, with more

than enough straw to give some of it up to a boy for his bed. Joshua piled it up in the corner best hidden from the door, and wriggled down into it, glad of the clean-smelling softness and warmth. The horse eyed him curiously, then settled back to its dozing. Joshua was just falling asleep himself when he was rattled awake by the quarter-chimes of the marketplace clock nearby. The horse paid it no mind, but Joshua heard every chime for the rest of the night, counting each hour until five struck, and he knew he had to move on, even though the sky held no light.

He cupped a hand into the horse's water bucket, regretting he'd taken no food from the farm, then slung his pack, patted the horse his goodbye, and emerged on to Church Street once more. The occasional early riser now was about, so he walked as casually as he could, down to the bridge and across. He waved a cheery 'good morning' to the bridge keeper, huddled in his hut, then turned on to the quay, slowing his walk so he could scrutinise each of the ships tied up there. The tide was rising, and although each vessel had just one man on deck, for harbour watch, he knew they would soon be busy with movement. There wasn't much time.

There were several whalers in amongst the fishing vessels and the colliers, and judging by the stores strewn on deck, the second was the closest to leaving, but Joshua had no way of knowing when that would be. Her deck was well below the level of the quay, and the watchman would surely spot him coming down the ladder, from his brazier by the fo'c'sle. Joshua stepped back from the quayside into the shadows once more. He knew what he had to do, and he had to muster his courage to do it. He slipped the compass into his hand and watched the needle swing in a diminishing arc till it pointed north, beyond the bridge, to the sea. The whaler's bowsprit pointed that way too.

'*Spero meliora*,' he muttered, as he replaced the compass in its pouch, then tightened the straps on his pack, took a deep breath, and set off at a run, straight for the edge. He moved as fast and as quietly as his clumpy boots would allow, directly towards the whaler's mizzenmast, and launched himself into space, desperate not to look down at the sliver of oily water between quayside and hull far beneath his feet.

The ratlines of the mizzenmast rigging met him with a blow at least as hard as anything Hestall or Flint had flung his way: but his bitter lessons in taking his beatings silently paid off now, for he uttered not a sound, while his legs and feet scrabbled for purchase on the slippery rope. As soon as they had found it he lay as still as the graves on the hilltop he'd passed, eyes flicking over the foredeck below till he spotted the watchman. Joshua was amazed that the old sailor had heard nothing and was even now busy with his pipe. He watched him a long time to establish the routine of his tour of the ship, counting slowly while he checked hatches and lights and mooring lines, before returning to his brazier. On each lap of the deck he passed beneath Joshua's perch, so close that Joshua could stretch his foot out and tap him on his oblivious head.

Close by, and astern of the ratlines, a ship's boat was slung in davits. By stretching and swinging Joshua thought he could just reach it. He waited till the watchman was in the bows, leaning over the rail, then made his move. He loosened the lashings, which held the tarpaulin stretched across the boat's top, and pushed his pack underneath. He wriggled after it into the cramped space below, criss-crossed with bench seats, oars, harpoon staves, and other bits and pieces he could neither recognise nor name.

Slowly and carefully he manoeuvred himself into a space at the bottom of the boat, where he curled up with his pack under his head and wooden frames digging in everywhere. He was exhausted, but still could not sleep, for now the sounds of a wakening ship rang out around him, and the lightening sky showed through the holes and eyelets in the tarpaulin cover.

He still didn't know the ship's name, but soon knew he'd chosen correctly, for the activity about him was just like that he recalled so well from the *Lindisfarne* a year before. He sensed movement as she was warped along the pier, and listened to the shouts of farewell from the gathering crowd on the quay. He pretended they were calling to him, as he had called out to his father. 'Three cheers for the *Aurora*,' they yelled from the end of the pier, in what to Joshua was a kind of christening. *Aurora*. He liked her name.

As the sails unfurled, one by one, he felt the ship slowly rouse into a life of her own. She started to lift to the wind, and roll with the waves. Then, in time with her roll, came a new sound, out of place somehow here on the water: the clanging of a bell, coming closer. Joshua shivered and frowned at the mournful tolling, till he realised it was Whitby Bell Buoy, marking the approach to the harbour and the dangerous rocks to the east. Waves sweeping past the buoy sounded the bell in a slow and steady funeral rhythm, as if the ship were a hearse, and this, its boat, a coffin, bearing him away in a train of farewells. Farewell and good riddance to Hestall and Flint, and to Laurence. Farewell and thank you to Esther. Farewell, with love, to little Emmy and ever-faithful Nelson. Farewell to Whitby, and the farm, and all the world he knew. Joshua would hear no farewell for his father. He was setting off to find him at last, however long it took and however hard the looking.

The bell's doleful clangour faded away astern as the ship lifted faster and started to heel. The water surged and hissed past the hull below, singing up to him, and bringing with it at long last the blessed release of sleep.

Part 2

Stowaway

Chapter 10

As the *Aurora* sailed on, and the Yorkshire coast fell away, the growing North Sea swell made her pitch and roll in an uncomfortable corkscrew motion, which seemed amplified inside Joshua's dark confined space. He braced himself as best he could against the thwarts of the boat, almost thankful he'd had nothing to eat or drink for a long time: but even so he felt the seasickness grow within him, as a cold queasy churning in his empty belly. A little rainwater had found its way through the tarpaulin, and sloshed about in the boat's bilges below him. He dipped a hand in it and rubbed it over his forehead and neck, and then tasted his fingers. The taint of tar and paint was unmistakable, but he had to drink something, so he spooned it awkwardly up to his mouth, wondering how long he could lie there, before he was forced to declare himself.

A sudden thwack on the boat's planking, close by his head, was followed by a roar from the deck below. 'Out o' there, ye little skulk-skin. Out o' there at once or I'll whip ye raw.'

Joshua was stunned. How could they have found him so soon? Further thwacks and roaring forced him into scrabbling the tarpaulin undone. As soon as he emerged, blinking, from the boat, he was grasped roughly by the arms and hauled down to the unsteady deck. He suddenly felt cold.

Two men faced him while others looked on from the rigging. One of the two, who looked somehow familiar, held a boathook's cruel glinting tip under Joshua's chin, and grinned menacingly through blackened teeth. The other, who seemed to be in charge, stood back and looked Joshua up and down. 'Tie him to the shrouds,' he said. 'I'll tell the captain.'

The black-toothed sailor shoved Joshua to the port bulwark and tied him to the mainmast's rigging with harsh twine, which he seemed to enjoy pulling tight. Catching the stink of his rotten-toothed breath rekindled Joshua's seasickness, so that sweat prickled across his cheeks.

'Scared, are ye?' growled the sailor. 'And rightly so. Know what we do to stowaways?' He didn't wait for a reply, for he had spotted the strap of the compass case around Joshua's neck. 'Well, well,' he cackled, as he pulled the case from inside Joshua's shirt. He started to undo it, his bloodshot eyes ever wider with greed, until Joshua could bear it no more. He lifted himself by the bonds on his arms, drew both legs up and kicked the sailor in the chest.

The blow was not a strong one, but the surprise of it made the sailor stagger backwards and lose his footing. A snarl contorted his ugly face when he got back up, and he rushed towards Joshua with his boathook raised.

'That's enough!' A sharp command halted the sailor in his tracks. Only when Joshua saw the boathook set down did he look at the voice's owner. The captain was not as tall as the mate who stood beside him, or as thickset as the sailors nearby: but something in his manner made him obeyed. He held Joshua and the sailor in a cool and steady gaze, sizing them up. 'Speak,' he commanded, quietly.

'I found 'im, Captain,' gabbled the sailor. 'A stowaway and a thief, who bears his haul about his neck.' Now that Joshua could not resist, the sailor slipped the compass from its case and held it up. 'A Scoresby compass, Captain. Stolen goods for sure.'

'Indeed,' said the captain. He was watching Joshua closely. 'Well?' he asked.

'That I'm stowaway is plain, sir, but thief am I none. This compass was my father's and now is mine. I'm returning it to him.'

'And your father is?'

'Thomas Murphy, sir. Specksioneer on the –'

'– *Lindisfarne*. Which has been beset.'

'Or worse,' hissed the sailor, under his breath, so only Joshua could hear. Joshua glared at him, more in anger now than fear. Rumours of the *Lindisfarne*'s fate were clearly spreading: but he would not hear them from a man such as this, especially when he seemed to relish it so.

'Unleash him,' said the captain. Two nearby crew complied. As Joshua rubbed life back into his aching wrists, the captain came closer. He looked down, stern but not harsh, and spoke. 'I know your father, lad, and you are not alone in wanting some firm word of the *Lindisfarne*. But this is a whaling ship, not a rescue vessel to ferry stowaway boys to the north.' He handed back the compass. 'We will put you off at Orkney. Until then you will work your passage.' He turned to the tall man beside him. 'Starboard watch, Mr Hobbs.' The tall man nodded.

The captain made as if to walk away, then wheeled on the black-toothed sailor. Now he *was* harsh. 'And his rations will come from your share till then, Wisely, since it was during your harbour watch he came aboard, was it not?' Suddenly Joshua knew why the sailor looked familiar: he'd seen the top of his head pass just below his feet, time after time, while he hung in the rigging. Wisely slunk away, casting baleful glances at Joshua.

Mr Hobbs watched the captain go below, then glanced from Joshua to his whaleboat hiding place. 'Been in there a while, eh? Hungry, I'll warrant?' Seasickness and hunger fought for control of Joshua's stomach. Hunger won: he nodded. Hobbs pointed forward. 'Go down to the galley and tell the cook from me you're to have a little bread and salt beef. And I mean a little. Then report back to me: starboard watch is mine and I will see you work your keep, right enough.'

Hobbs kept his word. Joshua was used to work, but, two days out of Whitby, he barely had strength left to reach his hammock when the watch-end bell sounded. Soapstoning the deck, sweeping out the fo'c'sle, fetching and carrying

galley stores, polishing brasswork, washing dishes – the tasks followed each other in an endless
round. At first he was slowed by seasickness,
especially below decks, but Hobbs sensed this
and set him work above whenever a swell was
running.

He was lodged in crew quarters in the fo'c'sle,
where space was so short he had to sleep above
the table, and could only sling his hammock
when the meals were done and the dishes dealt
with. The sailors were glad to have him do these
chores, but grumbled at their reduced space, and
took little care not to bump him as he swung in
sleep in the middle of their cabin.

Joshua avoided Wisely as best he could, and
was ever grateful the captain had assigned him
to the opposite watch. He knew Wisely wouldn't
try anything with others around, or in open view,
but once, as the port watch squeezed past his
hammock, Wisely's foul breath and lizard hiss
wafted over him, and a clammy hand tugged at
the strap of the compass case. 'I'll have this, and
I'll have you, boy, before Orkney. You'll not land
there unmaimed.' Joshua asked Mr Hobbs to
entrust the compass to the captain for safe
keeping soon afterwards.

Exhausted though he was, Joshua knew he
couldn't risk sleep when the fo'c'sle was empty,

and he spent increasing off-watch hours out on the bowsprit when the crew weren't working there. He lay along the thick pine spar, arms and legs locked into the rigging, and watched as the bow below cleft the grey-green waves into a boil of foam. Excitement bubbled within him as the ship sped ever northward. They could put him off at Orkney if they liked, but he'd never go back to Whitby. He'd find another ship and another and another, and keep going north till he found his father or there was no more north left.

Hobbs had not assigned him sailing duties, but Joshua already knew the name and function of every buntline, halyard, sheet, downhaul and brace, from close observation of the crew and how they managed the sails. One bright morning Mr Colbeck, the second mate and leader of the port watch, called to him as he stared upwards. 'Want to do some climbing, lad?'

Joshua wasn't sure. It seemed so far, even to the lower yards, and the masthead traced a great arc across the sky as the ship rolled. He knew it wasn't a question, so he swallowed hard and nodded. 'Aye, sir.'

'Then up you go.'

Joshua swung on to the ratlines, clinging tightly in the very spot where he had first leapt aboard. It was very different with the sea rushing past below. He craned his neck. 'How far?'

'To the top.'

Joshua started climbing. He told himself not to look down or even up, just straight ahead at the ratlines that he grasped. When the ship rolled to port, and he hung backwards over the sea, he clung on tightly, and when she swung back to starboard, he climbed, gingerly, methodically, stiffly, one hand or foot at a time, and always keeping three points anchored. The ratlines narrowed, the higher he got, and they were soon clapped close against the mast. He paused.

'Up,' came Colbeck's voice from below.

Joshua frowned. Up, yes, but how? He looked backwards to see the narrow ratlines slanting behind and above him, to round the overhang of the cross-trees at the topsail yard. To get to the platform, and the safety it offered, he would have to reach high above his head and climb almost upside down, using ratlines tied so tight he could hardly slip a foot between them. He breathed in deeply and stared ahead, waiting for a big wave. He saw one and told himself that it was his: and when the wave rolled under the ship and pushed her over to starboard he scrambled up and back and over the lip, till he first knelt and then stood on the platform of the cross-trees, thankfully gripping the mast and wiping the sweat from his brow.

'Up again,' called Colbeck.

This time it was even more difficult. The ratlines were narrower, and rose more steeply, and every foot of height he gained magnified the ship's movement, so that the seasickness he thought had passed began to rise again. His arms and legs trembled, telling him he was gripping too tight, but it was hard to relax when he looked down to an unforgiving wooden deck flanked on either side by the surging sea. He imagined himself falling, and wondered whether it would be better to crash to certain death on the foredeck or into the water; there to bob while the ship sailed obliviously on, leaving him to the mercy of the sea and whatever lived in it, miles from the nearest land.

Enough. Joshua shook such thoughts from his head and climbed on. Soon he was at the topgallant cross-trees, where he could seek rest once more. Far below he saw Mr Colbeck waving: but instead of the distant 'Up again' he feared, there came a reprieve. 'Well done, lad. If you make the crow's nest you may rest there then descend for some grog.'

Joshua peered upwards. Fixed to the mast ten feet above him was a barrel, with a hole in its base just wide enough for a man's body. When he reached it, he wriggled easily through, then closed the hinged flap which sealed the hole shut. He stood within the barrel, shielded from the wind and trying to tell himself his shivers were due to cold, not fear. There was a movable canvas hood, which he could swing against the wind for more shelter still. He smiled, as his seasickness ebbed and he delighted in the view. It was *magnificent*.

Behind and below, ochre-red sails bellied outward in wind-swollen curves, restrained by creaking ropes. Before him stretched a wide and sail-free horizon, with, to the west, the dull smudge of land laid upon it. There were no other vessels on view, but the waters nearby were carved apart by the great sweeping strokes of a dark scimitar fin-shape, as a solitary dolphin circled the ship again and again. It cavorted in the bow-wave, then disappeared with a thrust of its muscular thrush-speckled tail, only to re-emerge by the stern, so close Joshua could see its blowhole open and close, in fast fishy clouds of breath. It seemed to relish in turn the role of a jockey, a companion and a gad-fly to the stolid shape of the ship, before boredom took over and it vanished in a flash.

All Joshua's seasickness and fear disappeared

as he watched, entranced. At length he grew tired and cold, and, sensing the approach of the bell to mark his watch, he knew it was time to descend. It was so much quicker and easier to go down, but even so Joshua welcomed the touch of the deck beneath his feet.

'Here, lad. A spot o' grog to mark your feat.' Mr Colbeck stood by a heavy wooden grog tub, and held out a porcelain beaker. An evil-smelling liquid swirled darkly within. Sailors clung to the rigging and stood about the deck. One of them was Wisely. Joshua saw this was some kind of test: he took the beaker and downed its contents. There was a pause, then an explosion of coughing and spluttering, as a kind of fire surged down his throat and into his belly. It burned and burned until he thought it would not stop, and all the while, as he spluttered, the sailors' laughter rang in his ears.

When eventually it eased, Joshua straightened, and looked up at Colbeck, through eyes that would not stop watering. 'Thank you, sir,' he said. 'Must I have grog every time I go up?'

Colbeck and the sailors roared, but with a different laughter now: all except Wisely, who didn't laugh at all. Colbeck tousled Joshua's hair. 'Nay, lad. Just t' first time.' Colbeck took him by the arm and led him to the stern, where Mr

Hobbs was detailing the starboard watch duties. 'But now 'tis your watch, and you must work.'

As the watches changed over Wisely brushed past and jarred shoulders with Joshua, knocking him against the helm-wheel. A knife flashed briefly, disappearing in an instant as another crewman came astern. 'Before Orkney, boy,' Wisely spat as he made off, eyeing the grog tub as if it were the holy grail.

Chapter 11

In the days that followed, Joshua spent every available off-duty hour in the crow's nest, unbidden by Colbeck or anyone else. The sailors did not begrudge him this rest, for they had come to respect his hard work when he was on watch. Climbing up grew easier, though it still had its heart-in-mouth moments: but Joshua knew they were worth it. He loved it aloft, lulled by the woody warmth of his sunlit chamber and the rolling movement as the ship rode the light swell.

He would listen to the captain or mate far below, calling out the course, and soon learnt that he always knew what it was – immediately, instinctively, unerringly – whether or not he caught the cries of 'Nor' nor' west' or 'East nor' east,' as the ship tacked up the coast. So strongly did he feel in his bones the pull that came from the north, that, without thinking, he oriented to it constantly, no less than did the swinging needle in the steering compass on deck below.

He would test himself when the helmsmen changed over each hour, and the course was confirmed aloud. He would whisper along with the new helmsman when he called to the watch commander. 'Nor' east, Cap'n.'

'Nor' by west, Mr Colbeck.'

'Nor' east by east, sir.'

Not once was he wrong.

He assumed he shared his instinct with all sailors – but he was keen to learn its limits. One sun-sparkled forenoon, with some free hours between breakfast and his afternoon watch, Joshua loitered near the quarterdeck for the change of helm. He wanted to test himself again, this time at deck level. He stared out to sea as Wisely stepped up to the great wheel, then closed his eyes to concentrate. 'East nor' east,' he whispered, in chorus with the outgoing helmsman.

'East nor' east,' replied Wisely, dully. When Joshua turned back, Wisely was staring at him. He was as hostile as ever, but the rat-like sharpness in his gaze had gone, and his eyes were now bleary and bloodshot.

Joshua shuddered and went forward to the foremast shrouds, where he waited for an approving nod from Mr Colbeck before he clambered up. Colbeck grinned. 'Aye lad, but on watch or no, I want sharp eyes aloft, for we pass the Bell Rock this day, God willing. I want you to sing out loud and long when you sight the lighthouse. It should be well off to port.'

Joshua waved back his willingness, and climbed up to the nest he now thought of as his, and not belonging to any crow. He settled into the barrel, and scanned the glittering sea for any sign of lighthouse or land: but saw nothing. The wind was a soft south-easterly, and the ship rode the low swell with ease, sailing free on a starboard tack. It was a beautiful day. He swung the canvas hood behind him, laid his forearms on the barrel's lip, rested his chin upon them, and gave himself up to his daydreams for the first time since leaving Whitby. Thoughts of his father were never far from his mind, but now that he was working his way north to him, he had less need and less energy for building the pictures in his head that had kept his hope alive all winter. Now they returned, in visions of icebergs, stranded ships, and a crew, led by his father, hailing rescue. Their cheers drowned out the half-heard barking of a forlorn dog, far behind in the south; a different vision Joshua tried hard to shut out.

A vague unease stirred him from his reverie. He surveyed the horizon: all was as before, but his uneasiness failed to settle. He glanced below, where Wisely still held the helm, while Mr Colbeck supervised the fitting of harpoon heads on the foredeck. Joshua frowned: something wasn't right. He looked around again, and closed his eyes, and then he had it – they were off course! East north east, they'd said . . . but the wind had shifted, and Wisely had let the ship come round with it, several points to the north.

More anxious now, he scanned the horizon again. There was nothing to see but a thickening haze off the port bow. Should he go down and tell Mr Colbeck? Should he shout? Either way it would make Wisely even more furious. And just what was it that made him so sure, anyway? What would happen if he was wrong?

He looked down again. Wisely scowled back, drew one finger unsteadily across his throat, then extended his arm to point directly at Joshua, with an evil leer on his face. His chilling gesture silenced Joshua, who resumed his horizon lookout. Fear lodged in his stomach like a lump of cold porridge.

The haze off the port bow approached rapidly, thickening all the while into fog as it came on. Suddenly they were in it, and Joshua's unease grew. If they had meant to pass the Bell Rock to port, but had drifted off to the north, then it could be getting uncomfortably close, now that they could not see. The Bell Rock had a fearsome reputation. He'd heard his father tell of a returning whaler, full of oil and happy homecoming sailors which was wrecked there some years before.

But no one else on the ship seemed to share his concern: they all trusted Wisely and his helming. Joshua twisted round and round in his lofty perch, straining his eyes for any thinning of the fog, and his ears for any sound above the creaking of rope and wood and canvas.

When he next looked down and could no longer see Wisely, he made up his mind to act. He bent over the barrel lip and screamed at the top of his voice. 'Mr Colbeck! Mr Colbeck! We're off course! We're too close to the Bell!'

Muffled voices spoke below, then Colbeck called up. 'What's that, lad?'

Joshua summoned all his breath, cupped both hands to his mouth and yelled. 'Hard a-starboard, sir! Hard a-starboard! It's the rock!'

A dim figure sped to the helm, hurled aside the dimmer figure of Wisely, and spun the wheel. The ship heeled hard, and Colbeck shouted a string of orders. Men sprang to the braces to haul the yards around, shouting to each other and back at Mr Colbeck.

All the noise suddenly stopped as the fog cleft apart to reveal the razor sharp reef and its sentinel lighthouse, sweeping past the port bulwarks, so close Joshua could see through its windows.

The shouts below doubled in urgency, as the crew worked to bring the ship round. 'Heave boys, heave for your lives.'

Joshua cowered helplessly in his barrel, banging his head against the side and telling himself over and over, 'I should have said, I should have said.' He clamped his hands over his ears to shut out the next noise that must surely come: the terrible splinter of timbers, as the *Aurora* struck the cutting teeth of the hungry reef.

But instead the shouting died, the fog thinned, and the bustle on deck lost its panicky edge as the crew came to see they were safe. The rock and its lighthouse fell away astern. Joshua slumped in the barrel, trembling and cold. He was startled by a rapping on the barrel's base. 'All right, lad?'

came the voice of his watchmate, Bob Barrow. 'Come on down. I think we all need that grog this time.'

Trembling with shock, Joshua was glad of the sailor's help, and the renewed warmth of the sun on his back as he descended to the deck. He was led astern and placed before the captain. Mr Colbeck still had the helm, while Wisely cowered by the bulwarks, blood trickling from a head wound. It could have been accidental: or equally well inflicted by any one of the angry sailors who crowded the deck.

The captain rested a hand on Joshua's shoulder. 'Well done, lad. Well done indeed. We owe you our lives and our ship. But for your sharp eyes we should surely have been wrecked.'

'Thank you, sir,' Joshua stuttered. 'But I didn't see it before anyone else.'

'Then it must be your ears we should thank.' The captain tousled Joshua's hair, straightened up, and turned away.

'Nor did I hear it sir, try though I might.'

'Oh?' The captain stopped, and turned back to face him. 'Then how?'

'I just knew, sir. I knew we were off course, and had been for some time. I was sure of it, but afraid to say.'

The captain drew up to Wisely. 'Well?' he asked.

'He's lying, Cap'n. There's no way he could know. It was the set of the tide swept us on to the rock, sir.'

'And nearly to our deaths, Wisely.' The captain screwed up his nose, then his face clenched suddenly tight. 'But by the smell of your breath I'd say it was more a tide of grog that put us in peril, you damnable drunkard.'

He wheeled round to the first mate. 'Confine him in the hold, Mr Hobbs. In irons, if need be.'

Wisely snivelled as he was lead away. 'Please, Cap'n. Please.'

'Enough, you grog-sponge!' For the first time the captain's voice was raised. 'Ask me no more! You were a fine sailor once, till drink addled your brains. My memory of those days, and my sympathy for your poor family were what had me take you on this voyage, much though I now regret it. Your days on this or any other Whitby ship are done. Now get out of my sight.'

Wisely was taken below. The entire crew watched the captain, who would not meet their eyes. He walked stiffly forward, to rest a hand on the foremast and gaze upwards. He moved on to the bows, where he patted the bowsprit, then came slowly back to the quarterdeck. Joshua watched his fingers trail absent-mindedly along the rail, until he stooped before him again, all the anger now gone from his face.

'Now, lad, tell me how you did it.'

'I just know where north is, sir. I don't know how.'

'Really?' The captain looked up as the first mate returned to the deck. 'A blindfold, if you would, Mr Hobbs.' A scarf was wrapped around Joshua's head, covering his eyes, and tied tightly at the back. The captain spun him round two or three times, then stopped him sharp. 'Point north,' he commanded.

Without hesitation, Joshua indicated with an outstretched arm. Mr Colbeck's voice from the helm confirmed that he was right.

He was spun again, this time the opposite way. 'Again,' said the captain. Joshua indicated. 'He's right, Cap'n,' said Mr Colbeck, to a murmur from the rest of the crew.

This happened over and over, in the bows, at the stern, amidships, even briefly, below decks, to satisfy Mr Hobbs that it wasn't the sun, or the wind, or the roll of the ship that Joshua navigated by. The spinning was increasingly elaborate, the captain sometimes moving with Joshua, sometimes the opposite way, to confuse him further – but every time Joshua's arm shot out, Mr Colbeck's voice answered with increasing admiration: 'Right again, sir.'

Eventually the blindfold was removed, and Joshua blinked at the faces around him. 'Extraordinary,' said the captain. 'A marvel.' He rubbed his chin. '*Joshua*, did you say? Well, henceforth we shall call you Compass. Compass Murphy.'

The group of astonished sailors broke into raucous applause. 'Three cheers for Compass Murphy,' shouted Mr Colbeck. The sailors' hearty response rose in a rapid crescendo, accompanied by broad smiles and so much vigorous clapping of his back that Joshua's shoulders hurt. When at last they had stopped, and returned to their duties, or their bunks, Joshua looked around the vessel he was already coming to love, and then the wide horizon. For the first time since his father had gone he was happy.

Chapter 12

Joshua straightened to ease his aching back. The deck he was scrubbing rolled under his knees, as a large swell swept in from the west, driven across hundreds of miles of Atlantic Ocean by some now-blown-out spring gale. To port there was nothing but open sea and the setting sun, whose reddening rays gilded the huge Hoy cliffs off to starboard. Joshua stole landward glances in between his scrubbing, as the ship drew in closer to shore. His looks grew more frequent and more astonished as there emerged a stunning sight: a huge finger of rock rose sheer from the seething sea for hundreds of feet, to dominate the cliffs behind it. The middle was wider than its narrow sea-girt foot, so it looked as if it must surely fall, and it tapered again towards the flat but sloping tip. The swell burst repeatedly at its base in explosions of spray, which rose to meet the writhing clouds of seabirds circling the summit.

'It's the Old Man.' Mr Hobbs's voice behind him startled Joshua back to his scrubbing, at least till Hobbs laughed. 'Nay, lad. Not t' captain. Yonder stack o' rock. The Old Man of Hoy, they call it. And old though it be, and frail though it looks, it'll outlast you and me.' Joshua's father had mentioned it to him, and spoken of a wager that he would climb it one day. Looking at it now, higher than he had ever imagined, Joshua vowed that he would climb it too: but only if his father was with him.

The bell on the quarterdeck rang out. 'Enough, now, lad, there's end on t' watch. And a good job too, for if you'd scrub same patch o' deck much more you'd wear it clean through.'

Joshua cleared away his bucket and brush, then pointed up the foremast. 'May I?' he asked, scarcely waiting for an answer before he scrambled up the rigging.

From the crow's nest the Old Man and the cliffs beyond looked just as high and even more forbidding, despite the warm red-gold hues the dying sunlight burnished on to them. Joshua watched as the cliffs grew ever higher and darker in the fading light, troubled by thoughts he could not voice.

The sun had gone when the *Aurora* rounded the northern end of Hoy, and turned east in to Hoy Sound. With the swell and the wind behind her she surged forward along the glittering blue path cast by a near-full moon. Low-lying islands lay ahead and on either side, with the lights of farmhouses scattered across their velvet silhouettes. The moon lit up a ghostly beach off to starboard, shimmering bone-white and coral-pink.

The port watch worked quickly in the rigging near his nest, reducing sail to slow the ship. They were directed in their duties by the firm voice of the captain and not, as usual when at sea, by Mr Colbeck, who now had the helm. More and more lights were coming into view, and then, quite suddenly, a whole cluster of them appeared to port, as they passed the headland which hid the town and harbour of Stromness. A huddle of houses were strung along the water's edge, off to the north, with lights brightly blazing. In the harbour, the braziers and lights of a throng of ships answered the shore display opposite, and the stars above, in a bobbing constellation.

Joshua gasped at the beauty, desperate to be among them to find his next vessel, but his heart sank when he heard the captain below. 'It's busy in there, Mr Colbeck. We'll not get in this night, even with the moon.'

He took the ship on, under almost no sail now, then turned her windward and let loose the anchor. The bay was well sheltered, and the ship slipped slowly sternward, in what little wind remained, until the anchor bit. Joshua stared ahead at the thickets of rigging. There were so many ships. Even if none had word of the *Lindisfarne*, he had to find one bound north before the captain put him on another heading south. He mulled this over till Mr Colbeck called up; 'Come on down, Compass Murphy. There's food here to mark our landfall.'

Despite his fears for his father, and his doubts about the quest on which he had embarked, Joshua was usually so tired by the end of his watch, that he fell asleep the moment he reached his hammock. Tonight, though, the knowledge that he must soon quit the *Aurora*, and steal aboard another vessel kept him awake.

Perhaps Wisely had wailed just as much on previous nights, and had not been heard over wind and wave: but now, in the stillness of the bay, Joshua could not rid his ears of the pitiful moaning down in the hold. Wisely seemed tormented by visions and nightmares, which only eased with daylight – but by then Joshua was up and ready and waiting.

'Can I go ashore to find a ship, sir?' he asked Mr Hobbs, as soon as he stepped on to the quarterdeck.

The captain strode briskly up from his cabin just after Hobbs. 'I don't recall you asking permission to come aboard, young Murphy; but go ashore you may. Join the watering party in the gig.' He indicated one of the rowing boats which was being lowered behind him. 'And when you have found your homebound vessel, I want you back here to tell me her name and that of her master.'

Homebound, thought Joshua. This way he might not have to lie, for home was with his father, wherever that was, and not, as the captain implied, down south back in Whitby.

'Your compass I will keep as forfeit lest you do not return,' the captain said, coolly. 'For I fear you, like it, point only north.'

Joshua knelt in the bows of the gig, penned in by empty water casks. Behind him sturdy oarsmen plied the boat towards the shore. The tide was high, allowing them through the narrow passage between the tiny islands which marked the eastern limit of the harbour, and the shoreline, where a single seal lolled. As the gig passed, it rolled into the water and vanished, only to re-emerge by the bows, startling Joshua as its dog-like head rose above the water to stare straight at, if not through, him.

The seal soon saw its quest for fish scraps was futile, and left them. Joshua looked up at the jumble of rooftops that made up Stromness. Thick-walled stone houses, little-windowed against the winter winds, turned their gable ends to the water. Many had their own rough stone piers and slipways, and brightly-coloured boats lay scattered about. Curls of peatsmoke lifted from the chimneys, to be wind-stretched across the harbour.

Joshua stared at every vessel they passed, mumbling their names and home ports under his breath, in a bid to consign them to memory, and trying to pick out the whalers for special attention. Within minutes he'd identified the *Caledonian* from Dundee, the *Kittiwake* from Hull, and the *Isis* from London. There were many more, but these looked his likeliest prospects, if only for now. Mixed in among them were fishing vessels of every size and type, an idle passenger ferry, and what looked and smelt like a cattle boat. Rowing boats plied between ships and shore like worker ants tending a whole nest of queens, and shouts of recognition and banter rang back and forth, sending up a babel of accents to shatter the still air of morning.

The gig tied up at the pier, and Joshua stood aside as the men unloaded the heavy casks and the wooden stretchers on which to carry them. Mr Colbeck, who had helmed the gig across, left in search of the harbour master. Bob Barrow rolled an empty barrel on to its side and tapped it with his foot. 'Here, lad. Roll this 'n down to t' well along wi' us.'

Joshua rolled the barrel noisily off the wooden pier and on to the stone-flagged quayside. He followed the sailors as they turned into a narrow street that wound its way parallel to the shore. Steep passageways ran off either side: up the hill on the right, or down to the water on the left. He caught flashes of sparkling water, wheeling seabirds, and russet sails. Joshua, reminded by all this of Whitby, was looking about too much to pay proper attention to his barrel, which rolled off ahead, bumped down some steps, and ran over the tail of a dog as it slept in a patch of sun-warmed stone. It ran off, yelping loudly, to

Joshua's shame and the laughter of his colleagues. 'He'll be glad it weren't full,' one of them shouted, and the rest of them laughed again. Joshua, suddenly thinking of Nelson, didn't join in.

They finally stopped at a low stone wall, with a square entrance the size and shape of a window set into it, but at ground level. Joshua rolled his barrel up to the wall and upended it, then peered through the opening at the darkness within. 'Login's Well,' said Bob Barrow. 'This water's been all around t' world, with Captain Cook. And now we've to load our share. 'Tis heavy work son, so you may be about your business. If you're to be askin' about ships, try the harbour pilots up at the Ferry Inn. Only mind you're back at t' pier by dark.'

Joshua retraced his steps, studying the inn signs, until he found the Ferry Inn, near the pier where the gig had tied up. He stood at the door, looking around, and was briefly alarmed to see no ship where the *Aurora* had anchored, until he spotted her masts swinging southwards past the islands to enter the harbour itself. Joshua turned back to the door, knocked loudly, and walked through. Eight pairs of eyes swung across, as he stood framed in the doorway, and eight laughing mouths fell silent, till the woman behind the bar spoke at last, in a sing-song lilt Joshua had never heard before.

'Looking for your father, is it?' Joshua was astonished: how did she know? 'Well? Do you see him here?' She indicated the men. Some stood at the bar, drinking already. Others sat more seriously, wreathed in tobacco fumes and the aroma of coffee, studying newspapers or working at scrimshaw. Joshua took these to be the harbour pilots, skilled sailors who rowed out to incoming ships, and guided them through the shoals and tidal streams into harbour. The woman resumed. 'No? Well away and tell your mother if he's not at work, then 'tis some other inn he bides at, and if so I'm as put out as she.' The drinking men, but not the pilots, laughed briefly, as if they were indulging her.

Joshua held his place. 'Indeed I seek my father, ma'am, but all I hope to find here is word of him or his ship.'

The woman exchanged glances with the men at the bar, then imitated Joshua's accent. 'Anyone understand him? He speaks proper strange.' They laughed again, then turned away and ignored him.

A heavily bearded man near the door ushered Joshua in. 'And no doubt we speak strangely to you, lad.' Joshua nodded. 'Name the ship.'

'The *Lindisfarne*, sir. A whaler, out of –'

'– Whitby, bound for the Straights fishery, a year ago. Aye. I piloted her into Hamnavoe myself. I remember marking her out for the way she had men at the pumps all the time.' He saw a cloud of worry darken Joshua's face, then sought to dispel it. 'Recent work on her timbers, the skipper told me. Wood not swollen up yet, like a new-launched ship.' Joshua looked in his eyes, trying to fathom their depth. He didn't like the sound of this.

The pilot looked away, into the fire. 'Well, she's not been back, nor any news of her but rumour neither, and if there'd been any we'd know it. She took on Orkney men here, see.'

Joshua felt chilled despite the fire behind him: all he'd learnt of the *Lindisfarne* was that she had been leaking. He'd been prepared to hear nothing – but this was worse, however the pilot dressed it up. When he spoke again his voice trembled. 'I'm to ask for passage on a south-bound ship. Do you know of any?' He listened intently, while the pilot rattled through the entire harbour of ships. He knew the names, the home and destination ports, the owner and master, and the dates of sailing of every single one, only once seeking confirmation from his companions nearby: and even then he was right. Joshua pretended to listen to the roll-call of south-bound ships, but ticked off, on out-of-sight fingers, the names of all the whalers going north. The name *Caledonian* came up twice, and he decided she'd be his next ship.

Armed with this information, he returned to the shore, to scout out how he might reach her. Already the *Aurora* lay to at the pier, and her crew were busy exchanging empty water barrels on deck for full ones on the pier. The captain seemed even more eager than the other whalers to be heading north quickly: Joshua knew he'd have to make his move that night.

He paced restlessly back and forth along the quayside until he saw the captain and Mr Hobbs at the stern rail of their ship, staring directly at him. The captain lowered a telescope to his side. Joshua backed into a narrow passageway, then turned and climbed quickly upwards, away from the water. The thick-walled fishermen's cottages stood close on either side at first, but soon gave way to farm buildings set back amidst small fields. Climbing higher, the path petered out amid thick tussocky grass, studded here and there with outcrops of granite, and divided into geometrical shapes by dry stone walls made of the same grey stone. Flowers of every colour blazed around his ankles as he neared the summit, and with each upward step the wind hit him harder.

He explored the hillside till he found a sheltered hollow overlooking the harbour, savouring its name – Hamnavoe, the pilot had called it – and here he settled down to watch, and think, and wait.

If he was discovered in his attempt to board the *Caledonian*, all the northward progress he'd made towards his still-distant goal would count for nothing. And if he did get on board, could he count on finding again the charity he'd been granted on the *Aurora*? What if it was a whole crew full of Wiselys? And the captain a Hestall? Joshua shuddered, but he knew there was nothing for it but to take his chances. He would swim across, and scale the ladder he'd seen at the *Caledonian*'s stern, and then find somewhere to hide. After that he'd be back to hoping. It had worked so far.

Chapter 13

He was woken by a gunshot, and sat up sharply, looking about wide-eyed till he worked out where he was. A puff of smoke at the shoreline to the south marked a cannon's placement, and he could see, near the solitary gun, a little knot of people waving joyfully at a ship coming into the bay. There was an answering puff of smoke from her deck, followed a moment later by another report, quieter than the first. In the streets below people emerged from the houses and shops to thread their way down to the quay in a happy buzz. Children's shouts lifted up to him, getting louder as the ship drew in. Joshua covered his ears and turned away. There was only one ship whose return he wanted to greet.

The sun had already dipped behind the summit of the hill. Joshua was surprised he'd slept so long. He puzzled over the broken fragments of dreams that returned to him. Cold fingers of wind at the back of his neck. Voices in the long grass. Water rising above his boots. A huge and fearsome seal charging head on at his gig. None of it made sense.

He shivered, shook the pictures out of his head, and set off back downhill. The harbour lay in shadow as he approached the pier. He still didn't know what he was going to do.

Mr Hobbs stood by the *Aurora*'s gangplank. 'Aha!' he said. 'Consorting with witches, eh? I trust you paid her for a fair weather spell?' He was enjoying Joshua's puzzlement too much to explain himself, and followed him up the gangplank till they stood on deck. 'The captain wants to see you.'

Joshua hesitated.

'Now.'

Joshua went astern, noting that Mr Hobbs stayed by the gangplank to bar his way ashore. His mouth was dry and his palms were moist when he knocked on the captain's door. 'Come in,' he was commanded.

Anxious though he was, he couldn't help take

in the details of the cabin. It was smaller than he'd expected, and simply but comfortably furnished. Charts lay scattered on the table, under a collection of brass instruments which gleamed in the candlelight. One of them was his compass. More books than he had ever seen lined the walls, and in the corner, above the bunk, was an etching of a woman and child.

The captain was making an entry in the ship's log. He looked up. Joshua searched his face for sternness or anger, but found neither. 'An odd place to find a ship, young Compass Murphy.'

'Sir?'

'Up on Brinkie's Brae there, in the witches' hollow.' He reached out and tapped the telescope in front of him with the side of his quill. 'We were watching you.' He dipped for more ink. 'Well?'

Joshua was silent. The scratching of the captain's pen filled the cabin. 'Southbound ships. You were to bring me the names of vessels and their masters, were you not?'

Joshua gabbled through the list he had memorised, hoping he'd got it right, while the captain scratched on. When Joshua stopped, he laid down his pen, picked up the compass and fixed Joshua with a steady gaze. 'And those going north?'

Joshua swallowed, and opened his mouth to speak.

The captain hushed him with a raised hand. 'A boy who has watched twilight fall from a witches' hollow had best not tempt fate with untruths, would you not say?'

Joshua closed his mouth.

'I'll wager you know the northbound ships only too well, and unless we confine you, you will be on one this night.'

Joshua looked at his feet.

'I'll wager also that if it means abandoning your precious compass, your only tangible link with your father, for the frail hope of finding him, you would do that too.'

Joshua looked at the compass and then at the captain, who seemed to know him better than he knew himself. He nodded.

'I like your spirit, lad. But I will not have you discovered as stowaway on some other ship in Greenland waters, when it is common knowledge that you came here on mine.' He opened a drawer in the desk and removed a heavy key. Sweat trickled cold down Joshua's back. To be confined in the dark beside a raving Wisely . . .

The captain thrust both key and compass into Joshua's trembling grasp. 'Here, take this key to Mr Hobbs. I want Wisely released and put ashore.' He stood up and turned to the window by the bunk. Joshua couldn't see if he was looking through it, or at the picture which hung close by. There was a long pause. 'You may stay on board. Better with us than any other ship in those waters. We leave at dawn. Now be off.'

Joshua was so overcome he clean forgot to thank the captain as he left the cabin. He beamed as he handed the key and the captain's message to Mr Hobbs, who waited still by the gangplank. Mr Hobbs seemed pleased, try though he might to hide it. As he turned to go below Joshua thought to ask him: 'You spoke of a witch, Mr Hobbs. The captain also.'

'Aye lad. Old Bessie Miller. Lived for years in a hovel up there on the hill, right where you laid your head. Any ship leaving harbour had to pay her to conjure fair winds. She never said she were a witch but she always took the money. She's long dead now.' He went below, leaving Joshua alone by the bulwark, and suddenly cold. He felt again wind fingers probing his collar, and a sigh in the rigging seemed to speak his name. He shuddered: if he'd known he would have avoided the entire hilltop.

The *Aurora* slipped her mooring lines the following dawn, and rowing boats drew her away from the pier. Joshua stood by the bowsprit, enjoying the sunshine and the familiar weight of the compass around his neck. He waved to no one in particular on shore. Four or five people waved back. Sails unfurled above as the ship got under way. At Mr Hobbs's command, he cast off the lines securing the rowing boats, and watched them drop astern. The men at the oars called a final farewell.

The piers and quays of Stromness slid past, and within moments the ship was turning west to round the low headland, which marked the entrance to the bay. Right on the shore, his feet lapped by water, stood a strange figure, waving madly. Joshua waved back, till he realised who it was, and he froze. Lit by the early sun, with darkening clouds behind him and lank hair streaming in the wind, was Wisely, blind drunk and raging. He scanned the ship till he saw Joshua, whom he fixed with a terrible stare. An outstretched bony arm pointed straight at Joshua's heart, and Wisely's shouts rose above the sea sounds, to be clearly heard by Joshua and everyone else on board.

'I curse thee boy! I curse thee to hell!' Strings of spittle flew from Wisely's mouth, as he splashed and stumbled through the shallows alongside the ship. There were more curses, in a language Joshua did not know, and then a final terrible spell, screamed across the water: 'You will find your father, boy, but you will wish you had not! A curse upon thee for ever!'

No one spoke, as the ship sailed blithely on. Joshua stared back at the shrinking figure on the headland, till Bob Barrow dropped a comforting hand on his shoulder. 'Fear not, lad. He's a drunken fool, and his curses count for nothing while you are with us.' But Wisely's warning rang in Joshua's head again and again as the *Aurora* sped towards Greenland.

Part 3

To the Heart of the North

Chapter 14

Three days out of Orkney, Joshua woke to an absence of land on the horizon and a different routine on the ship, which he puzzled over until the bell called the crew to their Sunday service. He assembled on deck with the rest, facing the quarterdeck aft, where the captain led the service, flanked by Mr Colbeck and Mr Hobbs. The men's hymn-singing was full-throated but unmusical, especially as it lacked any instrumental accompaniment, but it seemed to suit the setting. The background sounds of ship and sea and sail, the swooping flight of the following fulmars, and, above all, the soaring canopy of cloud-streaked pale blue sky, brought the hymns to life more than any fusty church, and Joshua joined in with gusto, whenever he could remember the words.

When it came to the sermon, Joshua's attention wandered, and he found himself fiddling with the compass case under his shirt, just as he had in St Mary's at Whitby. Emmy had sat beside him that day, he remembered, and Nelson had waited outside, tied up by the porch. *Spero meliora*. He'd felt the words on the compass, and seen them on the stone, and lived them for months now. Another word – *Wisely* – jumped out of the captain's speech and startled him, so that his compass clattered noisily to the deck. The captain paused, as Joshua scrabbled to retrieve it, hoping desperately that the glass was intact. The sailor in front of him scowled down and shushed him angrily. Joshua stood up. A glance was enough to tell him the compass glass was whole, and the needle seemed to swing just as before. He looked up, and only then did he feel the captain's eyes upon him.

'As I was saying –' the captain continued, 'you all know Wisely was put ashore at Orkney, and you all saw his pitiful state as we left. I'm sure you shared my anger that his wayward helming nearly wrecked us, and my relief that it did not.

I hope you can also feel forgiveness, remembering how our Lord spared Nineveh, wherein were not one but sixscore thousand persons that could not discern between their right hand and their left hand.' He paused. Joshua did not sense much forgiveness from the men around him. At his side, Bob Barrow's huge fist clenched tight. The knuckles were raw.

'Wisely's place in our crew has been taken by young Joshua Murphy, known as Compass. Though tender in years he has proved his worth . . .' Joshua glowed. '. . . even if he cannot hold a silence in sermons.' The glow changed to a burning blush.

The captain closed his book. 'We will end with Reverend Heber's hymn.' Joshua's heart lifted, for he knew every word of this one, and sang them out lustily:

> *From Greenland's icy mountains,*
> *From India's coral strand,*
> *Where Afric's sunny fountains*
> *Roll down their golden sand . . .*

Joshua cared nothing for coral strands or sunny fountains. He was sailing north to icy mountains, and though they might be Greenland's, they also belonged, in a way, to Whitby, and to his father. His voice rose as he reached the final verse, till he was almost shouting:

> *Waft, waft, ye winds His story,*
> *And you, ye waters roll,*
> *Till like a sea of glory*
> *It spreads from pole to pole.*

At dinner in the fo'c'sle afterwards, Joshua found himself hemmed in against the bulkhead by the sailor who'd glowered at him. He knew him as Edward Sumner, an unsmiling man, full of the bible, which he quoted from memory at every opportunity. The close quarters life they led aboard ship meant this was often. Usually Joshua walked away, but now, pinned in as he was, there was no escape if he was not to go hungry.

Clouds of steam curled up from the bowls of thick stew before them, to mingle with sailors' quick breath, as they blew on their heavy spoonfuls. Joshua had learnt the need to eat quickly on the farm: here he had to be faster still, even if it meant a much-burnt mouth.

Sumner didn't eat at all, but stared straight ahead, droning scripture. 'But the Lord sent out a great wind into the sea and there was a mighty tempest, so that the ship was like to be broken.

134

Then the mariners were afraid, and cried every man unto his god.'

'Ignore him,' said Bob Barrow. 'We all do. Sunday sermons get his fervour up – do they not, Edward?'

Sumner didn't even look at him. He was trembling so that his spoon rattled against his bowl, setting Joshua's teeth on edge. His voice rose, and now he turned to fix his eyes upon Joshua, 'Then they said unto Jonah, tell us for whose cause this evil is upon us? Whence comest thou?'

Bob Barrow broke in firmly. 'That's enough Edward. You're scaring the lad.' He signalled behind Sumner's back. Joshua immediately understood the gesture, and slid out from his seat on the bench, hastily spooning up the last of his stew. He grabbed a hunk of bread and his heavy jersey, and made for the door.

Sumner suddenly stood up and all the chatter at the table stopped. He was shouting now, face lifted to the ceiling overhead. 'So they took up Jonah, and cast him into the sea,' he yelled. Then he lowered his gaze to look directly at Joshua and lowered his voice to a cold hard flatness, like a knife. 'I hope you're not a Jonah, boy.' Bob Barrow shoved him back to his seat, and Joshua left.

*

Deepening cold had forced Joshua to abandon his stints on the bowsprit, except when engaged in watch-work. The chilling spray and cutting wind quickly turned him blue, whatever his inner excitement. He now measured the *Aurora*'s northward progress in the increasing layers of clothing he needed to make a turn in the crow's nest bearable, but the more he wore, the heavier and more awkward was the climb. He'd taken to making two trips, to ferry up enough clothes, but this time he didn't dare return to the deck and Sumner's ranting, so he huddled within his pendulum barrel until Bob Barrow appeared, looking over the lip. 'Cold, eh? You wait till we're in the ice.' He tossed in a bundle of heavy garments, some of which were his own. 'Here. These should help,' he said. Joshua quickly pulled them on, shivering his thank yous.

'Stay out of his way for an hour or two and he'll be fine. And put that Jonah nonsense out of your mind.'

Joshua nodded, and looked around for the first time since he'd come aloft. Seeing no land at all, his world felt, not expanded, as he'd expected, but suddenly smaller, shrunken to the confines of the little pod of life beneath him, bobbing solitary amid a vast expanse of grey-green sea.

Bob Barrow was already on the way back down. 'Keep an eye open while you're up here, Joshua. We're far from the whaling grounds yet, but sing out loud nonetheless if you spy a spout.'

Joshua was reminded again that the ship's mission was the same as his father's had been, and different from his own. Spout-spying gave him a focus, while he tried to do as Barrow had bade him, and banish all notions of being thought a Jonah. It was easier said than done: Sumner clearly saw him as some kind of jinx, even if the rest of the crew didn't. Not yet, any way. Superstitious Donald Lewis was always on about omens and signs – he'd been nervous when they'd shipped out of Orkney on a Friday – and Joshua wondered if he'd be next to take against him. He knew there was nothing he could do about it but hope Bob Barrow was right.

Once he could trust his thawing fingers to do as he wanted, he slipped his compass from its case and inspected it closely. It was working just as before – he realised he'd checked it against his own sense of north, and not the other way round. He could identify no new dents or scratches among the many it already bore. He warmed himself further by polishing it vigorously against his sleeve, till the reflections from the midday sun flickered into the shadowed depths of his crow's nest. Satisfied, he secured it once more, and set to scanning the sea, pulling a jersey half over his head, and retracting his hands deep into his sleeves.

Seabirds swept by, in various shapes and sizes. To those he recognised, he could apply the names he'd learnt from his father, like the fulmars which had followed all the way from Orkney: but mixed in among them were other, newer birds he could not name. He admired their mastery of flight as they dipped with the waves then rose to swoop past at crow's nest height, with hardly a flap of their wings. Joshua envied them their freedom. With wings like theirs he'd have been in the ice a year ago, instead of working a heavy ship northwards at little more than walking pace.

Chapter 15

Hours must have passed, though he had wandered so far across frozen landscapes in his day dreams that it could have been days: but something must have intruded to bring him back to the here and now. He scanned the whole horizon, shading his eyes against a sun now dropping from its zenith. There was nothing new to see. He scanned again, more slowly this time. Again nothing. Then once more, this time the opposite way, for variety.

Now he saw, away off on the starboard bow, a curious puff of spray and vapour, rising above the waves for some seconds, to disperse in the wind. Below it a dark shadow slipped lazily through the waves. Joshua frowned. When he stopped rubbing his eyes, whatever it was had gone. Had he really seen it? When it came again he leapt to the lip of his barrel. 'A spout! A spout!' he yelled, indicating furiously with his outstretched arm again and again.

The men below sprang into action like a team of horses whipped to a sudden gallop. Several leapt into the rigging, staring keenly where Joshua pointed. A great shout went up when they all saw the next spout together, but it was quickly stilled when they turned to see the captain on the quarterdeck, and they remembered he'd given a Sunday sermon from the same spot just hours before.

The captain looked around, taking his time. He folded his arms. 'Well?' he called, a half-smile on his face. 'Sabbath or no, gentlemen, we have a fish to catch. Look to it.'

Another shout went up. Mr Hobbs gave orders to put the ship round to starboard, and the working watch hauled hard on the braces. The opposite watch, roused from the fo'c'sle, dashed to lower and load the whaleboats.

Joshua jigged on the spot with excitement, and nearly jumped out of his barrel when a voice beside him spoke. He wheeled around, to see Nathaniel Bridge. 'Jonah be blowed!' he grinned, handing Joshua a bell. 'We can scarce hear you on deck, lad. Use this. We've turned to follow the fish. You watch him like a hawk, and ring where he goes. One bell, he's turned to starboard; two, he's turned to port. Three, he's dead ahead, four, he's making to dive. Got it?' Joshua nodded. 'Show me where he is now.'

Joshua pointed to patch of sea, a mile or more away yet, just to starboard of the bowsprit. They waited an age till the tell-tale breath came again, this time dead ahead. Joshua rang loudly three times. 'That's the spirit,' laughed Bridge, fingers in his ears. 'See the way his spout goes forward an' left, and puffs out wide?' Joshua hadn't, having no spouts to compare it with, but on the next puff he did, just as Bridge roared down to the captain below. 'Sperm whale, sir, an old bull I reckon, forty, maybe fifty feet.'

Joshua was astonished: he could tell all that from the spout? But when he looked around Bridge had already gone, and he next saw him on the bowsprit, a bell of his own in his hand.

The ship was drawing slowly closer, creeping up behind the oblivious whale as if in a deadly game of grandmother's footsteps. Joshua watched it closely. He'd never seen a live whale before but even so he knew there was something wrong. Its progress was slow and halting, and something in the way it moved its tail looked amiss.

The boats were lowered now, rowing after it and fanning out on either side. When the whale turned to port, to see the boats at last, and maybe to hear Joshua's frantic two-bell ring, it changed its manner. At first it swam faster, blowing hard, as if to escape, then abruptly it turned again, first dead ahead – three bells – then to starboard – one bell – then all the way round to face boats and ship head on. Joshua didn't know how many bells there were for this, so he rang continuously, till it was obvious all on board could see the creature for themselves and he need ring no more.

At first the whale just lay in the water, observing them all, like a stag at bay. Joshua marvelled at its huge size, even though he knew most if it was hidden from view. Its massive head rose out of the water to the height of the bowsprit, with little eyes set low on either side, just above wave height.

When he saw what happened next, Joshua froze in fear. He was fully expecting the whale to dive, and had his bell at the ready, when instead the monster set off at speed straight towards the *Aurora*, raising a foaming bow wave that rose to meet the curious star-shaped white patch on its head. His father had told him nothing about this.

'Fighting whale, sir!' shouted Bridge from the bow. The captain called orders to bear the ship away. Mr Hobbs spun the wheel while the sailors heaved on the braces as never before. The whale turned too, still trying to meet the ship, but this brought it closer to the lead boat. The oarsmen in it pulled furiously, urged on by the steersman in the stern. In the bows stood Bob Barrow, harpoon in hand. The boat and the whale closed rapidly, the whale so intent on pursuing the ship that it paid no heed to the smaller vessels about it. Bob Barrow waited and waited until it seemed he could reach out and touch the creature's back with his hand, never mind his harpoon. And then he struck, plunging the harpoon deep into the whale's side. It erupted in a tumult of pain and fury, thrashing its great flukes in a sea of foam. One of the boats was upended, spilling its crew into the chilly waters.

Joshua looked on, awestruck, as the creature broke off its pursuit of the ship and set off eastwards, towing Bob Barrow's boat behind it. The linesman behind Barrow worked frantically to pay out the line attached to the harpoon, in case the monster should dive, while the steersman struggled to hold a course, and the oarsmen did all they could to keep the boat from capsizing. Throughout all this Bob Barrow calmly prepared his second harpoon. When he held it ready he signalled his crew. They drew up closer to the great beast again until, when they were almost on its back, Barrow thrust his harpoon in with all his strength.

When the whale's next spout came it was a fountain of blood, which spattered down on to its back and Bob Barrow's boat like crimson rain. The whale thrashed for a while, while the fountain weakened, as the second boat drew up. Joshua turned away as they went to work with their harpoons and killing lances. He looked back instead at the capsized boat, now under tow back to the ship. Men were still being helped out of the water to flop like fish in the scuppers. Joshua counted heads again and again till he was sure all were safe, then glanced back at the whale, now lying limp in the reddening sea.

He heard the whoops and the excited shouting as the boats drew in, but he didn't share the sailors' joy, and began to regret that it was him who had spotted the spout. He might no longer be a Jonah to his crew mates, but he surely was to the whale.

Mr Hobbs hove the ship to, while the carcase was secured alongside, and the boat crews came aboard. Bob Barrow's crew was a terrifying sight, drenched in dripping gouts of blood, which matted their hair and clothing. With triumph-widened eyes and grins, and raucous laughter, they were a vision from hell. Bob Barrow, who was bloodied the most, ran straight across the deck and threw himself into the sea to wash it off. None of the others followed, preferring to clean themselves with buckets as best they could. Mr Colbeck hauled him back on board, chiding him for his foolhardiness and commending his success by turns.

When all were back on board, and clean, if not yet fully dry, the captain passed around the grog tub, and gave the wetted men a double share. Joshua didn't come down: he didn't like grog and was in no mood to celebrate. The captain proposed a toast. 'Our first fish! The first of many!' and when they had cheered themselves hoarse, and drained their draughts, the grog tub was stowed away and the terrible work of the flensing begun.

Two men on deck used sharp blades on long poles to strip the blubber from the whale's body, while two more did the same from a boat tied alongside. One man put on spiked boots, and stood right on top of the whale while he went about his butchery. They carved long strips of blubber off, and passed it up to the deck, where it was cut into smaller pieces and sealed in casks.

The sights and sounds and smells sickened Joshua, who could bear no more. He slumped in the crow's nest, realising with a shudder that it was no more than a barrel, and had probably held blubber from many a whale before ever it sheltered him. He tried not to hear the awful noises as the head was hacked off, the precious teeth prized free from the lower jaw, and the even more precious spermaceti oil drained from the melon, the mysterious cavity in the whale's bulbous forehead.

Just when he thought they had finished came another sound – the screech of metal on metal – from over the ship's side. He looked down to see the flenser, stood near the whale's tail, the only part of the animal that was still intact. He held above his head a broken-off harpoon, reddened by old rust and new blood. 'Captain,' he called, 'He's been pricked before.'

The flenser stooped to wash the weapon off, then passed it up to the captain who inspected it closely. 'No marks of identity, Mr Gavin. It could be from anywhere. Just be thankful we've had more fortune than they did.' And with that he hurled it into the sea.

When all the work was done, the mutilated carcase was cast adrift, the sails set, and the ship put back on her northwesterly course. The decks were sluiced with seawater, and the casks of blubber stowed, while Joshua watched the mangled lump of meat – the krang, they called it – as it drifted astern, staining the sea, and attracting a cloud of swarming seabirds. So this was how proud creatures met their end, he thought. Just hours ago, before I cried him out, he was a magnificent beast, a rightful ruler of the waves. And now he's just carrion for sea-crows. Father said nothing of this.

The sailors' loud laughter and the smells of their supper wafted up from the fo'c'sle, but still he didn't descend. He had no appetite for food or the company of killers. Instead he watched the whale's remains until the light began to fail and his shivers returned, then climbed stiffly down to the blood-sticky deck, and across to the fo'c'sle.

Most of the sailors were asleep, drowsy with food and grog and toil and triumph. Those who were awake said nothing to him. Joshua picked his way to his bunk and slid in. Even when he was warm again sleep would not come. Every time he closed his eyes he saw fountains of blood, or a thrashing wounded whale, and the harpooneer's silhouette in the whaleboat's bow was always that of his father.

Chapter 16

The following dawn saw a sleepless Joshua on deck, scrubbing away all traces, both real and imagined, of blood and blubber. He could only haul half-buckets of sea water, so heavy were they, so his refill visits were frequent, and on one he felt the captain's eye upon him. He turned to see him on the quarterdeck, as still as an extra mast. He must have been there a while; and he waited a long time further before he spoke.

'A fine job, young Murphy. But is it not a comment on my ship that you feel it needs to be cleaned, unbidden, and at a time when you are not on watch?' Joshua set down the bucket. He hadn't expected this.

'I will see you in my cabin when you are done.' The captain turned to go, but was stopped by a further thought. 'And, of course, you will not be finished until you have scrubbed clean those parts of deck where the whale was not.'

Joshua's scrubbing was less frantic now, distracted as he was by worry about what awaited him, and a wish to put it off; but as the morning wore on he knew he was expected. He emptied the last bucketful of water over the now pristine deck, dried his hands on his trousers, and went aft. The captain's cabin door was open, and he sat at his desk within, scratching at the ship's log. He looked up and beckoned. It was only when Joshua drew up to the desk that he saw the captain was not writing, as he had expected, but drawing, carefully inking in the outline of a whale's head in the left-most column of the big double page.

'What's this, Compass Murphy?' he asked. He didn't look up.

Joshua, who was not yet used to his new name, was mystified by the question. 'Why, it's – it's a whale, sir,' he stammered.

The captain shook his still-lowered head, and went on with his inking. 'No: it is not.' He looked up at Joshua's puzzled face. 'When it is in the water it is a whale. Here, in this book,' he tapped the whale's head with his quill, as if it were a feathered harpoon, 'it is a roof overhead, and shoes underfoot. It is food within and clothing without. It is doctors' bills, and not having to fear a pauper's grave.'

He laid down his quill and fixed Joshua with a steady gaze. 'Every man in this ship has a share in her catch. Not equal shares – though some would have it so – but shares nonetheless. So every fish we catch and kill means wages or wealth, according to our station.'

He signalled Joshua to come around the desk, and flicked back through the log's heavy pages. 'This is last season. Not a full ship, but we did well enough – twelve whales in all.' Joshua saw the inky heads flash past, too fast to count. 'Bob Barrow bought a new cow. Mr Colbeck re-thatched his roof.'

'A whole farm,' muttered Joshua.

'What's that?'

'That's why Father went with the *Lindisfarne*. For a farm.'

'I know, lad. He went back to sea to secure a future on the land.' He sighed. 'So it is. Every man among us hopes for better things.'

He paused, then continued flicking back through the log book. 'Two years before we returned to Whitby empty. A dry ship, not a single cask filled, though the good lord knows we tried.'

Joshua stared at the spinning pages. 'There!' he pointed, as a whale-head flashed by. This one faced downwards. 'There's one!'

The captain smoothed the page flat. 'Well spotted. Your eyes are keener than my memory. But see how he's head down?' Joshua nodded. 'It means we caught him but killed him too quickly, and before we secured him he sank, taking all of our hopes with him. Bob Barrow sold his old cow. Mr Colbeck's children went another two winters with water dripping in every time it rained. I . . . I had to take my eldest son out of the college. We lost three fish that way. And any share of nothing still amounts to nothing, however big it be.'

He closed the log. 'It's a bloody business, Compass Murphy, but it is our living. There are whales a-plenty yet to hunt, and it is not for sport we do it. No. It is too hard and too hazardous for that. Though was there not some sport behind those keen eyes when you sang him out to us? Eh?'

Joshua stammered and stuttered, but was saved from the need to reply by a knock at the door. It was Mr Colbeck. Joshua saw him differently now. 'First ice, sir,' he said. 'Two leagues west.'

The captain frowned. 'So soon?' Joshua's instinct was to bound up above, but he had to wait to be dismissed, and the captain, no stranger to icebergs, was in no hurry. He sat down, shuffled his papers until a large Admiralty chart came to the top, and he bent to study it. A pencilled line marked the *Aurora*'s northwards progress toward Greenland waters, studded at intervals by the Xs that marked the noon position fixes, like a series of stitches. The captain scribbled some quick calculations, made some measurements with his dividers, and marked another, lighter X. 'It's a long way south, Mr Colbeck,' he said.

'Aye, sir, and it's big ice too.'

'Then let's take a look, shall we,' said the captain, as he stood and reached for his telescope. Joshua followed him up on to the quarterdeck, and his eager gaze followed Mr Colbeck's outstretched arm till he gasped at what he saw. Some distance off the port bow lay a massive iceberg, blinding white in the morning sun. Its sides rose sheer from the grey-green sea, and ended in a crest carved at the corners into pinnacles by the sun and wind, so it resembled an icy abbey ghosting by. Between the pinnacles sun-melted icewater pooled in a bowl-shaped valley, to spill in a sparkling torrent two hundred feet down. A mist rose where it hit the surface of the sea, and even from this distance Joshua could hear a faint roar. He thought of Whitby church, and the way, in stormy weather, rain-water spilled on to gravestones from gargoyled gutters.

'A full lookout, I'd say, from now, Mr Colbeck,' said the captain as he lowered his telescope. Colbeck nodded and called out to the men of the working watch. One of them – Edward Sumner – broke off to clamber the foremast rigging and take up position in the crow's nest, which Joshua knew now belonged again to the ship and not to him. Since it was from there he had spied the whale, the sense of home he felt within it had already gone.

The captain guessed his thoughts. 'No more idling aloft, Master Murphy. You can take your turn as lookout with the rest, but when you do you will scarcely blink. You will scan the sea for icebergs as if your life depended on it.' He paused, then added quietly. 'Which of course it does.' He paused again. 'And should your stomach have you muffled, if you spy a spout, I trust that your conscience will speak.' Joshua stared at him, unsure if he expected an answer, until he was dismissed by Mr Colbeck. The captain's mind was already elsewhere.

Joshua huddled by the bowsprit, trying to remember when he had last felt warm. He looked round to see fields of ice in every direction, so no matter which way the wind blew it would be chilling. Still he spent hours on deck, gazing at the spectacle strewn about him, even at the cost of eyes too sore for sleep when he was done.

Ice in all its variety had held him in thrall in the weeks since he had seen his first iceberg. His father had described it, but no mere words could do it justice. It came in every shape and size, and many different colours, and it bore a range of names he'd come to savour. There were great icebergs, cruising about like wilful white islands: pancake-flat floes, pushed here and there by fickle winds, bergy bits the size of a house, brash-ice, pack-ice, and the dangerous growlers. Most of the ice was a brilliant white, but some was streaked brown or black or grey in its course down the distant glaciers. Some bergs glowed with a brilliant blue, or sometimes, when the light was right, a luminous green. The growlers had no colour at all, and lurked low and unseen, waiting for unwary vessels like outlaw thieves.

Joshua had expected the ice to be silent, and was surprised to find it anything but, for his father had said little about noise. In even the slightest wind the floes bumped against each other, rubbing raised edges until they looked like giant soup plates. In anything above a breeze the noise rose all around to a distant grinding thunder, with mysterious creaks and moans that filled his dreams. The icebergs bade their silent time, then spoke in sudden gunshot explosions, as huge chunks broke off without warning and crashed into the seething sea. Once, Joshua saw a distant berg, higher than the cliffs of home, cleave itself in two with a cannonade crash that was not so much heard, as felt, through the timbers of the ship. The worst noises were quieter: it was impossible to sleep, when, inches from his head, ice floes scraped their way along the hull, as the ship nudged them gently aside. He hardly heard this when on deck, but, down below, the sounds were coupled to, and magnified by, visions of an icy reef punching through the hull, and torrents of freezing water rising beneath him.

For many days now the *Aurora* had sailed back and forth along the edge of the pack-ice, and sometimes in its midst, copying above what the whales did below. Many spouts were spied, but only one whale taken. After it had been sighted, and the boats lowered, the captain summoned

Joshua to his cabin. He indicated the view through the small stern window. 'Which direction?' he asked.

Joshua spun to face the door – his north – then back to the window. 'South-west,' he said.

'Correct again,' said the captain, indicating now the chart laid out on the table before him. 'Now show me where we are.'

Joshua pondered. This chart was bare of the pencilled Xs and zig-zag lines he had seen on others, and gave him no clue. The shape of the coastline was familiar enough, and he knew all the names of the waters – Baffin Bay, Davis Straight, Lancaster Sound, Melville Bay – but he could only guess where within them they now were.

'I thought not,' said the captain. 'Your nose for north is a gift, young Murphy, and we owe it our survival. But it is not enough. A navigator must know where he is, as well as where he is going. Your father knew that.'

Joshua was stunned. 'He – he sailed with you?'

'He did, many years ago. A fine man. And another reason I did not put you off at Orkney.'

There was a long silence, throughout which Joshua stared at the chart. He knew he was expected to speak, but did not know what to say.

'So where are we now, sir?' he asked, at last.

'Here.' The captain's finger confidently planted on an utterly blank patch of sea, in the heart of Baffin Bay.

Joshua looked up. 'How do you know?'

'With this.' The captain picked up his sextant, an ungainly contraption of brass, and eyepieces, and hinged mirrors. 'And this.' He opened a padded wooden box to reveal the ivory face of a silver-cased chronometer, the size of a big pocket-watch. 'And this.' He leafed through a heavy leather-backed book, its pages dense with tables and tables of numbers. 'But most of all . . .' he laid the instruments aside and tapped his head, '. . . with this. Would you like to learn?'

Joshua nodded. It was better than scrubbing blood off deck. He listened closely as the captain started him on the basics of navigation, and concentrated as hard as he could on the strange new words – azimuth, declination – but it was complicated and taxed his attention to the limit.

Laughter alongside prompted an interlude. The captain got up to peer through his window, then turned to Joshua. 'There's a whale in. A small right whale. You may join us above or continue your lesson below.'

Joshua reached for the sextant and turned another page of the navigation tables. The captain smiled, on his way to the door. 'Very well. When your chronometer shows noon draw nigh, you will come on deck and show me how you take a sight. If you get it right I will tell you of your father's days aboard this ship.'

Chapter 17

Time passed, in which Joshua shut out the noises of the butchery overhead by going over and over again what the captain had told him about using a sextant. He practised repeatedly taking a sight on the sun, through the cabin window, until he began to feel the glow that comes with mastering something difficult and new. He didn't hear the silence above until an extraordinary noise intruded upon it, sounding like the roar of an unknown animal. Whatever it came from was not made of ice. He puzzled over it, until he saw with a start that noon was nearing fast, and he dashed for the door, a precious instrument carefully cradled in each hand.

He was astonished to find the deck empty but for Donald Lewis at the helm and the captain on the quarterdeck. 'Any later and you'd miss it, lad, so look lively,' he said. Joshua turned to face the sun and braced his back against the mizzenmast. When he raised the sextant to his eye the cold metal of the eyepiece chilled his cheek. After some hurried fiddling with smoked glass filters and brass vernier scales he had before him an image of the sun brought down to the horizon, and balancing on it as an egg upon a table. He was astonished how fast the sun moved through the sky when seen like this, and he had to keep adjusting the scale as the captain counted down the seconds to noon. 'Now,' he said. Joshua lowered the sextant and took its reading. The captain quickly checked it himself, then nodded at him. 'Well done, lad,' he said. 'Your next lesson will be to use this reading to deduce the longitude.'

Joshua's spreading smile was stifled by another blast of the mysterious noise that had rousted him up from below. It came from the ice close by, on the starboard side, but he could not see its source. The captain was giving nothing away, and Donald Lewis, a hardened North Sea fisherman, but a fellow novice to the ice, looked as puzzled as Joshua felt. There came a cry from the lookout above, who was unrecognisable in a conical hat: 'Ice party ho! It's a royal visit, Captain.' It was only on looking up that Joshua saw the huge garland that decorated the mizzen-mast top, made of woven strips of ribbon and paper and cloth, streaming its many colours in the cold polar air, which rose from the pack-ice pressed close on all sides.

The captain grinned. 'Then welcome them aboard!'

But the visitors had not waited to be asked. Over the starboard gunwale scrambled the oddest collection of creatures Joshua had ever seen. The first was a huge man, the size and shape of Bob Barrow, in a billowing sail cloth cloak, wearing a gilded crown from which straggles of seaweed fell to his shoulders. He held a trident made of a single harpoon stave and three harpoon heads, which he banged thrice on the deck before bellowing again. 'I am King Neptune!' he declared, to the captain's deep bow.

'And I am Mrs Neptune!' growled the not-much-smaller apparition beside him, wearing an improvised calico dress over heavy sea boots, bright red paint on its bearded cheeks, and a saucepan on its head, which wobbled when it curtsied. It made Joshua wonder what Mr Colbeck's mother had looked like. Behind was an array of vaguely familiar figures wearing some of the sail loft and most of the galley. 'And we are the Tritons!' they chorused.

The king spoke again. 'We bring Mayday greetings and seek tribute from your greenhorns. How many have you?'

'Just two, your majesty. The rest are polar men, good and true,' said the captain.

'Then send one below while we deal with the other.'

The captain handed Joshua the chronometer and sextant. 'Stow these securely, lad, and wait in my cabin.'

The last thing Joshua glimpsed as he went below was the captain taking the helm from Donald Lewis, who was dragged forward by Mrs Neptune and made to kneel at the feet of the king.

For what seemed an entire watch Joshua waited all a-tremble below, listening to the roars, the gales of laughter, and the thump of harpoon staves overhead. When it went quiet he knew his time had come, and sure enough, Mrs Neptune thrust her hideous head into the cabin. 'Time for a shave,' she growled, as she gripped him by the collar and dragged him up the steps.

There was no sign of Donald Lewis, but the deck was splashed with tar and paint and flour and water. Buckets of each stood about, either side of the main hatch cover, where King Neptune sat, enthroned amid his Tritons. The captain helmed the ship as if nothing unusual was happening.

'Would you be a polar man?' thundered Neptune.

Joshua could only nod.

'Then Tritons must trim your beard!'

'B-b-b-but I have no beard, your highness,' stammered Joshua. Before he had finished, three Tritons had splattered his face: one with tar, one with oakum, picked from old rope, and one with flour. Joshua spluttered and spat as the horrible stuff was laid on, while other Tritons held his arms.

'He says he has no beard, Mrs Neptune,' grinned the king.

Mrs Neptune brandished overhead the cook's biggest and sharpest boning knife. It flashed in the Mayday sun as she roared, in the voice of no woman, 'Then this is no razor!'

Joshua shrieked, wriggled free of the Tritons' hold, and rolled between their legs across the deck, knocking two of them over as he fled. He scrambled to his feet and was chased in circles round the foremast. Although he was grasped and grappled by flailing Triton hands, he was never quite caught, and the Tritons grew ever more breathless. Soon he found himself hemmed in at the bows, and retreating forward. He made a dash for the bowsprit before anyone could get behind him, and shuffled out along it until he reached the very end, where he sat astride it, high above the shimmering pack-ice. Somehow he had picked up a harpoon stave, which he now brandished before him as a Triton, as ugly as Edward Sumner, stepped on to the bowsprit. Joshua swished the stave to indicate his intent, but nearly overbalanced, and had to struggle to right himself. He locked his legs underneath the bowsprit and swung his stave again. The Triton shuffled closer, until he was just outside stave range. He looked at the harpoon swishing past his chest, then at the ice far below, and then over his shoulder to his king, for guidance.

But it was the captain, not the king, who spoke, and there was laughter in his voice. 'He has you, your majesty, unless your Tritons are to be dunked.'

There was laughter in the king's voice too, try though he might to hide it. 'But he must be shaved, if he is to be a polar man.'

'You cannot shave what you cannot catch, sir!' yelled the captain.

Joshua never took his eyes off Sumner, but called to his two-fold superiors beyond. 'Sirs,' he cried. 'Will I be a polar man if I shave myself?'

There was much conferring between captain's hat and Neptune's crown on the quarterdeck. Eventually they separated, and the captain called over. 'We say yes.'

'But –' shouted the king sternly, 'you must shave yourself with what you have to hand.'

Joshua made as if to scrape away the hideous mess that still clung to his face, using the wooden shaft of the harpoon. Immediately Sumner edged forward, and Joshua swished at him once more, this time at nose height.

'Polar men shave with a blade, lad,' said the captain.

'And that I will,' said Joshua, 'but I need this blade to keep a Triton at bay.'

At that the king called his Tritons back, and the whole ship's company, including a newly beardless Donald Lewis, gathered in the bows to watch as Joshua bent his head to the harpoon's sharpened sides. He swallowed hard when he saw on the blade what he took for dried whale blood, and then, very slowly, very carefully, he scraped the sticky mess from his cheeks. He tried to put aside all thought of what this blade, so close to his throat, might do if he slipped, but he was steady as a surgeon, until he was almost done. A swirl of wind shook the sails above him and swung the ship's bows so that his hand slipped and the cruel steel bit the side of his jaw. When he looked down he saw a trickle of his own fresh blood wash over the whale-blood stains, to drip on to the snow-swept ice below. Blood is never so red as when it splashes on snow, he thought, dabbing at his jaw with his sleeve.

The captain saw this too. 'That's enough, lad. Come aboard and we'll tend your wound, for you are now a polar man.'

Joshua grinned as he shuffled back along the bowsprit, to applause from all the crew. Mrs Neptune slapped a poultice on his face where he had been cut, and King Neptune handed him a mug. 'Polar man grog,' he said. Joshua wrinkled his nose, until King Neptune winked at him, and whispered in his ear, 'It's all right lad. I watered it down.'

Joshua joined in with the toasts, and then the singing (with toasts), and then, when the Tritons had given up their saucepan hats, with the food (with toasts again), until he was stuffed and sleepy and woozy and warm, and thinking that grog wasn't so bad after all. He climbed into his hammock, where he fell asleep in an instant, and swung oblivious to the carousing that continued for hours.

Chapter 18

There was no more carousing in the hard weeks that followed. The older polar men spoke of how the pack-ice was heavier than they had ever known, and the crew of the *Aurora* spent a great deal more time and energy in battling it than they did in catching whales. The frustration of spying spouts close by when the ship was jammed in was fierce, and grew fiercer still as the season wore on without any addition to the blubber-barrel tally. This troubled Joshua less than his shipmates, as all he wanted was to progress ever northward, and he spent his on- and off-watch time studying the ice that lay between him and the pole.

The days grew longer and longer until there was no night to speak of, and Joshua found himself aloft one midnight watch, astonished that the sun was still up. In the low grey-pink light he watched a mile-wide nearby iceberg in majestic motion. Driven westward by some secret current, it ran into and through light pack-ice, itself pushed east by a light but steady wind. The iceberg dealt with the pack-ice as if it was not there, scattering floes aside to pile up in clattering jagged confusion. Joshua was reminded of an oblivious carthorse in a yard full of chickens. He tried not to picture the fate of any ship caught before such a monster as this.

Several weeks and many hundred zig-zag miles later he swore he saw the same iceberg, this time lying still in nearly windless open water. Seals basked on a low shelf which extended from one side of it, and stared after the *Aurora* as she cruised slowly by. Joshua watched them, but older eyes watched the berg as they came abreast of it, and a cry went up from Mr Colbeck, 'She's rolling, captain!' at the very moment the seals noticed too, and hurled themselves into the sea, baying in terror. The iceberg, flung off its fragile equilibrium by the *Aurora*'s wake, now rolled as inexorably as before it had shunted pack-ice aside. Its after edge rose steadily, higher and higher, while on the other side, the seal-shelf dipped deeper and deeper. Water cascaded from its sheer and shimmering sides into a sea dotted with panicky seals, and still it continued to roll, further and further, until it came right round with a roar, setting up a great wave which rocked the ship. Joshua watched as it drifted astern till it was lost to view. When the *Aurora* tacked back to the north of it some hours later, it still swung back and forth like some enormous pendulum.

When the pack-ice closed in hunting parties went out on foot to shoot seal and walrus. This gave the hold blubber, and the cook some fresh meat, but most of all it gave the crew a purpose, and Joshua joined in keenly when he could. He minded this work less than the whaling, as the kill was cleaner. He needed the exercise, and he wanted to test his navigation well away from the ship. After so long on deck, it was strange to walk on the ice when he could still feel the swell of the water beneath.

Almost despite himself, he learnt he could find seals better than any of his crewmates, and though he left to them the killing, he shared in the heavy hauling of carcase-laden sledges. As they returned to the ship they often took detours to nearby frozen-in bergy bits to hack off great lumps for their water supply.

He was loading ice-lumps on to a sledge which already held two seals, when his normally taciturn workmate, Nathaniel Bridge, spoke up. 'I can make fire out of this, young Murphy,' he said.

Joshua looked at him, set his heavy ice-block down on the sledge, and said nothing. He was growing used to sailors' boasts, but this was a new one.

Bridge grinned. 'Don't believe me, eh?'

Still Joshua said nothing.

'I'll wager I can make your boots burn with nothing but this ice.'

'I'd accept your wager, Mr Bridge, but I have nothing I can stake.'

'Your tobacco, perhaps.'

'I do not smoke, sir.'

'I know. But you have a tobacco ration. Where do you think it goes?'

Joshua shrugged. It was the first he had heard of it. 'Wherever it goes you may have it if you make my boots burn,' he said. He lifted another ice-block, the last. 'And will you teach me scrimshaw if you fail?'

Bridge grinned again and held out a hand. 'Done,' he said.

Joshua helped him drag the sledge back to the ship, and watched as others hauled the seals and the ice on to the deck. Bridge took a block for himself, and chopped it roughly into something the size of a fist with his axe, and then whittled away with his knife till it resembled a swan's egg. He rubbed it in his mittened hands till it was smooth as a Whitby pebble and clear as glass. He kept stopping to hold it up to his gaze, staring through it at the world about him with a cyclops eye, until a grunt said he was satisfied at last.

He squinted at the sun, now high in the southern sky, and summoned Joshua. 'Your boots,' he said, tapping the hatch cover. Joshua bent as if to remove them, but was brought up sharp by a hand on his shoulder. 'Nay, lad. I want you to keep them on.' Joshua climbed up on to the platform.

Bridge held the lump of ice above Joshua's booted feet, and moved it here and there and back and forth, checking against the overhead sun, until he managed to focus the sun's rays in a brilliant pinpoint on Joshua's toecap. Within seconds the heavy salt-crusted leather blackened and cracked, and a thin curl of acrid-smelling smoke rose up before Joshua's fascinated gaze, until a piercing pain in his foot had him hopping around the deck amid much laughter.

'A wager won, I'd say,' Bridge gloated. 'And all your tobacco is now mine.'

Several nearby sailors were about to object, but were brought up short by a cry from above no one had heard for months now. 'Sail ho!' sang the lookout. 'Sail ho, I say!'

The entire watch followed the lookout's pointing arm, but from the deck saw nothing but ice. Joshua dashed to the starboard ratlines and scrambled upwards. Opposite, on the port ratlines, Mr Colbeck climbed up, too, but with rather more care, for a telescope was suspended from a lanyard he had slung round his neck, and he had not Joshua's reasons for haste. To him this ship would be a welcome fellow whaler, but no more. To Joshua she would be the first fellow whaler of the much-advanced season, and, given the merciless advance of time, perhaps the last. He hoped to heaven she was the *Lindisfarne*, and if not, that she would bring some news, some clue.

'Four points off the starboard bow,' said the lookout, once they had reached the level of the crow's nest. Joshua hung in the rigging as his hopes hung in his heart, but his eyes were too dazzled by ice-blink to see it yet. Mr Colbeck raised his telescope to his eye, and all was silent for what seemed a year, till he handed it to Joshua and called down to the captain. 'Aye sir, a sail for sure, and she's coming this way, through water more open than ours. I'd say she's a whaler much like us.'

Joshua scanned the horizon through the telescope, seeing at first only the jumbled pack-ice, then open water, with frost-smoke rising between the icebergs, and then, finally, like a tiny toy, a whaler. He strained his eyes for flags to identify her, but the telescope magnified his trembles so much all he could see was her sails. He handed the telescope back and listened for orders below.

Within minutes the *Aurora* had laid on full sail, and with the wind, and the muscles of the men, the captain endeavoured to free her from the pinching pack-ice. Joshua flung himself into this work as hard as he knew how, and when the large floe before them cracked across and the ship surged ahead, he grinned till his cheeks ached.

He continued to work the ship with his watch, but was not the only one to cast glances ahead, or to smile, each time he did so, at seeing the other vessel a little nearer.

An hour's heavy work left no room for doubt: the *Aurora* was making progress through lightening pack, towards the other vessel, who must have seen her too, for a flag was run up on her mainmast head. Joshua, who could still see all the flags the *Lindisfarne* flew as she left port, could not yet make it out. He broke off his hauling to stare astern, where Mr Colbeck stared back at him and held out the telescope. 'Go and join the lookout, my keen-eyed lad, and sing us out what ship she is.'

Joshua thanked him, slung the telescope lanyard round his neck, and scuttled up to the crow's nest. He locked both legs and one arm in the rigging as best he could, and lifted the telescope. He fiddled with the focus until an image of startling clarity leapt up the telescope tube. He could make out the sailors working on the other vessel's deck, just as his crewmates did below.

She was unmistakably a whaler, with a deck layout much like the *Aurora*'s, but something different in the lines of her hull made him quell his hesitant hopes. He could not make out her name, either in the gold lettering on her bows, or the upturned stern of the whaleboat on her deck, but something told him it would not be the *Lindisfarne*, and he felt a bubble of heavy emptiness burst within his chest. He raised his glass to scan her masttop flags, which was enough to tell him she was British, but no more. He lowered the telescope to rest his eye, and looked down at the quarterdeck, where expectant faces were raised to his.

He took up the telescope again, staring intently at the vessel's bows through thinning frost-smoke. Her name might not be the one he wanted, but he had been sent aloft with a job to do. When he was sure, he called down, working as hard as he knew how to put some life into his voice, though there was little left in his heart. 'She's the *Phoenix*, sir.'

Mr Colbeck cupped a hand to his ear and shook his head. 'We can't hear you, lad.'

'They'd hear him in Whitby if she were the *Lindisfarne*,' said the captain.

'Aye, sir, right enough,' said Colbeck.

Joshua looked down at captain and mate conferring below, suddenly sure they were talking about him. But he would hear no pity, and now found voice enough to do his duty. 'She's the *Phoenix*, sir,' he yelled. 'And a whaler, I think out of London.'

'Then back on deck and make ready to gam, lad,' said Mr Colbeck. Joshua's heavy-hearted progress back down was so slow that the *Phoenix* was within hailing distance when he handed the telescope over. Both vessels were soon hove to, and drifting side by side, a hundred yards apart, each with a rail lined by waving sailors.

After some shouted greetings a boat was lowered from each ship. The captain detailed Mr

Colbeck, Bob Barrow, Donald Lewis, Nathaniel Bridge and one or two others to man the *Aurora*'s boat, while he stayed on board to receive the *Phoenix*'s captain. Colbeck was the last to leave. He climbed over the rail, then turned to face the deck as he settled his feet on the rope ladder slung over the side. He caught sight of Joshua, low in the foremast rigging, apart from the rest. He opened his mouth to speak, but the captain had anticipated him.

'Compass Murphy!' he shouted. Joshua was startled. 'No true polar man would pass up his first gam. Get in the boat!'

Chapter 19

Joshua followed Mr Colbeck down the ladder, and picked his way forward to the only empty seat, next to Nathaniel Bridge, who nodded as he sat down. The little boat was quickly under way, but before they had gone far Bob Barrow, the steersman, stood up and addressed Joshua. 'We have three oarsmen on either side, young Compass, but, however hard I steer, we shall go in circles as long as only two of those on starboard row. So lay on.'

Bridge thrust an oar into Joshua's grasp. 'Watch, and follow,' he said. Joshua struggled with the heavy blade, its handle worn smooth by all those who had worked it before him. He followed the broad back of Donald Lewis in front, and copied the arm action of Nathaniel Bridge beside, and before long began to feel the rhythm, though every time he got it wrong he was hit in the kidneys by the oar of the man behind him.

Just as he thought he was picking it up, some underwater monster grabbed the end of his oar. The handle dug into his midriff and pinned him backwards against the gunwale, knocking the breath out of him.

The *Phoenix*'s boat drew abreast at this very moment, and a crew man called over in a strange accent. 'Wotcher, mate! Catchin' a Greenland crab are ya?' The other oarsmen laughed.

Bob Barrow cursed as he had to put the rudder full on against Joshua's dragging blade. 'Twist it!' said Nathaniel Bridge. But, try as he might, Joshua was still stuck.

'Oi'd say that Greenland crab's caught 'im,' said another of the *Phoenix* boatmen, with an even bigger roar of laughter. Joshua gritted his teeth, and put all his strength into twisting his blade as Bridge was trying to show him, and it suddenly popped free, showering him and Donald Lewis in freezing water. They rowed on, Joshua trying not to hear Lewis muttering about what would have happened if he'd stowed away on a London ship.

There were no more accidents in the rest of the short trip, and the boat soon bumped against the *Phoenix*'s port quarter, where a ladder hung down. Joshua followed his boatmates up on to the strange yet familiar deck, where they were heartily greeted by a throng of sailors, all talking in the same odd way he had just heard.

Joshua hung back, unnoticed amid the handshakes and the cries of ' 'Ey-up!' and 'All right mate?' all about the deck, until Bob Barrow pushed him forward. He rested his huge hand on Joshua's shoulder as he spoke. 'And this is our navigator. We call him Compass because when he's about we don't need no needle.'

The sailors laughed, but in a friendly way.

'He's all right,' said Nathaniel Bridge.

'For a stowaway,' added Donald Lewis, whose hair was still wet.

'Will you show us, lad?' asked Bridge.

Joshua looked at him steadily, realising he *did* have something to trade after all. 'Only if you teach me scrimshaw,' he said, firmly.

Bridge shrugged. 'But I have no skill for it.'

'You wagered it before,' Joshua replied. 'Against my tobacco.'

One of the *Phoenix*'s men pushed forward. His face was beardless and resembled old leather, it was so darkened and cracked from squinting into polar suns and blizzards. Strange tattoos covered his hands and disappeared up his sleeves, and an earring sparkled underneath his tight dark curls. Joshua would have marked him for a gypsy, were it not for his piercing blue eyes. 'Oi know scrimshaw, and will show you, boy,' he rasped. 'After.'

Bob Barrow took off his neckerchief and tied it round Joshua's head as a blindfold. Joshua was put through the same spinning and pointing tests as before. It seemed so long ago now, but the result was the same: right every time. The *Phoenix* men were amazed, but the *Aurora* party, some of whom had won bets on him, looked almost bored.

When the blindfold came off Joshua started at the scrimshaw man bending close before him. He held out a hand, and his stern face cracked into a brilliant smile. His teeth were so white the missing ones showed more. 'You 'ave a gift, boy,' he hissed. 'Be sure and use it well.' He straightened and turned to face his crewmates. 'But oi tell ya, north is one direction we'll not go no more. Not for a long old time, eh lads?' There was much shaking of heads and murmured agreement. He turned back to Joshua. 'Oi'm Clark. And oi will show ya scrimshaw, before ya go, whether it's to the north or not.'

In the hubbub that followed, Joshua learnt that the *Phoenix* was a full ship, now homeward bound. Her crew all said the season's end would be early, if it was not already upon them, and muttered darkly about their trials in the unusually heavy ice and storms to the north. Joshua never found the moment to put the questions that gnawed within him, and decided to wait, as the group split up.

Mr Colbeck and Bob Barrow went aft with the *Phoenix*'s mates and bosun, while Joshua joined the rest in the fo'c'sle. They squeezed around the table, sitting on sea-chests and empty barrels, while a thick stew was ladled out and supplemented with freshly-baked bread. Joshua listened to the banter flying about his head, trying hard to hear any mention of the *Lindisfarne*. But there was none, and he came to think that the question would not be put while he was in hearing, however much his crew-mates might share his concern for her fate. He had to hope the captain would ask the *Phoenix*'s skipper, and break it to him later, if there was anything to tell.

In a lull in the talk he caught Clark's eye, just as he wiped his bowl clean. He set the bowl aside and whipped out, from different pockets, a small slice of ivory sperm-whale tooth, a vicious-looking jack-knife, a tiny pot of squid-ink, and a grubby red cloth. He cleared a space on the table and bade Joshua squeeze up close to watch.

First he rubbed the already-smooth tooth smoother still, then he dipped a twisted corner of cloth into the ink and smeared it over the creamy surface, blowing on it till it was half-dry. With one powerful hand he gripped his little slab of ivory, and with the other his huge knife. With a delicacy unexpected, he scratched with the very point of the knife, through the ink and on to the tooth. The work was too fine for Joshua to make out, so he sat back to watch the intense concentration on Clark's face. When the ink dried completely he wiped it off, briefly revealing the lines and curves he'd etched, before more ink obscured them and he set to his craftwork again.

Another *Phoenix* sailor, introduced earlier as Mitch, leaned across and muttered to Joshua. ' 'E caught that whale 'isself, son. Years ago, dahn in the suvvern Ocean. That's the only bit what's left.' He turned to Clark. 'Far end of the old earth from 'ere, innit mate?' Clark pretended not to hear. Mitch laid his hand on the table with his fingers spread, and whispered conspiratorially in Joshua's ear: 'But 'e's more popular there, see. Known by name to all them penguins, innee?'

There was a whirl of motion, too fast to follow,

as Clark jumped up and his arm snapped down. His jack-knife slammed into the table-top, and stood upright, quivering, its tip embedded in the narrow space between Mitch's third and fourth fingers.

There was silence in the fo'c'sle, broken only by the creak of the rigging aloft and the lingering tremor of the knife. Everyone looked at Clark, their eyes flicking between his impassive face and his hand, which hovered near the knife handle like a hunting hawk. Only Joshua looked at his other hand, which was a clenched fist, tight on the table, sliding slowly across to him. Other eyes saw it as it lifted off the table, the only movement in the whole cabin, then came to rest against Joshua's chin. The much-scarred fingers slowly unfurled, like an ancient clam shell giving up its treasure. Inside, shining like a pearl, was the little piece of scrimshaw, now wiped clean of ink.

Joshua swallowed hard and looked down, all eyes now upon him. The whole fo'c'sle saw his eyes widen and heard him catch his breath: for Clark had carved him a compass.

In another flurry of movement, Clark slipped the scrimshaw into Joshua's grasp, retrieved his knife, and left. Joshua set his trophy on the table, the better to admire it, while Mitch spoke up, looking from one *Aurora* man to another. ' 'E get's edgy when the whalin's done. Says 'e can't stand the thought of comin' back, a full ship, and a fortune awaitin' 'im, only to 'it a rock or some other trouble wivvin sight of 'ome. As if it's worse to drown a rich man than a pauper, eh?'

Joshua rubbed his new compass smooth. 'But what set him off was your talk of penguins,' he said, absent-mindedly.

Mitch and the other *Phoenix* men laughed loudly: the *Aurora* crew merely smiled. 'We rib 'im abaht it. 'E usually takes it better. 'Im and some of us others 'ave whaled in southern waters as well as up 'ere. And in the southern ice, these funny little birds what walk on two legs are all over. Some of 'em not so little neither. Only, they 'ave this call, see, and it sounds like 'is name. "Clark!" they go. "Clark!" every time 'e's on the 'elm. We fall abaht laughin' because there's not a fing 'e can do abaht it. Not until 'e's back in 'ere any'ow. As you'll see by our table.' For the first time Joshua noticed that the table was studded with deep cuts like the one Clark had just made. 'I reckon 'e whales in the north to get away from them penguins.'

Bells sounded above, signalling a change of watch and an end to the gam. There was much shaking of hands and wishing of luck and promises of 'See you next year!' till the *Aurora* men went above to return to their boat. Joshua still hadn't found a chance to ask his question, but he saw Clark by the rope ladder, and drew him aside as the others clambered down.

Joshua held out his scrimshaw compass and looked into ice-blue eyes. 'This is very fine, Mr Clark, and I thank you for it. But I would return it in an instant if you could give me instead any word of another Whitby ship, missing in these waters a year now.'

'The *Lindisfarne*?'

Joshua nodded.

'I know of 'er. But I seen nor 'eard nuffink. We've been 'ere weeks now, and 'ave gammed before wiv other ships. Always 'er name comes up, but answers do not. I fear she is lost, lad.'

Joshua said nothing. His fist curled around his scrimshaw and he climbed down into the *Aurora*'s bobbing boat to take up his seat and his oar. He pulled away with the rest, and embedded himself in their rowing rhythm by repeating a chant, through gritted teeth, over and over, and in time with his stroke. 'Not . . . lost,' he hissed, as his blade flashed in and out of the steel-grey water. 'Not . . . lost. Not . . . lost. Not.'

Chapter 20

The two whaleships sailed easily east in company overnight, both skippers waiting for the wind that rose around them to open up the ice. Early the following morning the *Aurora*'s crew were assembled on deck. Already the *Phoenix* was sailing south, and many an envious glance went in her wake. Joshua gazed after her too, though not in the hope that he would soon follow.

'Gentlemen,' the captain addressed them. 'You have seen that the ice this year is thick, and the fishing all too thin. We have little blubber in the hold, and even less time before winter closes in. But the *Phoenix* you see now heading home found whales a-plenty not far north, and I have resolved that north we shall go.' A murmur of concern ran round the deck. Joshua tried not to smile. 'And we will turn for home not later than a fortnight hence, whatever the state of our catch.' Another murmur. 'Now let's to work.'

There was much muttering on deck that day. Some of the men wanted to go south at once, fearing a cold and fruitless winter trapped in the ice, while others wished to take the risk for the whales they hoped to find. They argued the score back and forth, though all knew it made no difference, for the captain was decided. Only Joshua felt gladdened to the core, for north was the only direction he sought, and if they should be iced in, so much the better. He had no idea what it would be like, or what he could do there to further his search for his father; but he could not face the thought of turning south, to Whitby and waiting, then stowing away once more in the spring. And if they did not chance upon her in the next two weeks, then there'd be another winter in the north for the *Lindisfarne* and all aboard her, whatever the *Aurora* did. There were few, if any, who had survived more than one winter frozen in. Joshua had to hold fast to *Spero meliora*.

The ice now came in bands, and in the open water between they soon found the riches their captain had promised. After landing three whales in a week the doubters were silenced. In between they worked the ice, day and night: poling off growlers, shouldering aside floes, and dodging big bergs. Twice they had to lay out ice anchors in a gale, and spend anxious hours fending floes away from their precious rudder. Once the whole crew worked through the night, cutting an ice channel and hauling their ship through it into another whale-laden lead.

After ten days of this, anxiety grew all over the ship like the ice-rime which thickened round the rigging in the ever-lower temperatures, until, one noon, the captain found himself taking his sextant sight, more closely watched than usual. He disappeared below to work out the fix, then returned to the deck, as they knew he would. 'Our furthest north, lads,' he said with a smile. 'Let's go home.' A huge cheer went up – though not from Joshua's throat – as the helm went over, and the men worked with a vigour renewed.

Within a day they knew they had left it too late. A steady breeze from ahead had packed the floes in tight around the ship, and the pressure began to build about her. From the crow's nest there was ice-blink in every direction, and not a trace of the frost-smoke or water-sky that might indicate open water. After two more days of the same southerly breeze the floes were rafting up, one on top of the other, and not far off a great pressure ridge was building. At night Joshua listened intently to the noise of the ice. Sometimes he heard the rumble of summer thunderstorms, or the roar of surf on Whitby rock. Once he woke to the guns of a passing frigate, and another time the whistle of an approaching train. He grew used to it, as long as it was far off, but the bangs and groans close by, and especially the creaking of the ship itself made sleep impossible. Each morning they awoke to ever-thicker ice about the ship until, when it was obvious to all, the captain called the crew together once more.

'Gentlemen.' He was not smiling this time. 'We are beset.'

Part 4

Beset

Chapter 21

The hard-packed snow squeaked underfoot as Joshua strode out. There was almost no wind, but the bitterly cold air pinched at the exposed parts of his face, and the hairs in his nose tickled as they froze. As long as he kept moving he'd stay warm, he thought, as he looked over his shoulder to check the little hunting sledge that slid silently behind him, attached by a harness like a dog on its lead. Criss-crossed on his back were a cut-down harpoon and a gun, which Bob Barrow had handed him that morning as he'd stepped on to the ice.

'For the bears,' he had said, before showing him how to use it, and warning him never to touch the freezing metal with bare hands. Joshua had heard the sailors talk of the great white bears of the north, but as he had not yet seen one himself, he felt more excitement than fear as he set out on his sealing trip. The rest of the crew were hard at work lowering the masts and laying them over the deck as a kind of shelter, and none were free to join him. The successful hunting parties he had joined were usually two or three strong. Now, with an urgent need to lay in stores for the long dark winter ahead, Joshua had a chance to show what he could do on his own.

He stopped to look around. As the freeze-up deepened over the month they had been stuck, the hunting parties had to wander further and further from the ship to find the open leads of water where the seals hauled out to rest or popped up to breathe. They were drawn ever closer to the forbiddingly jagged peaks of the Greenland coast. The light and air played strange tricks with distance: sometimes Joshua felt he could almost touch these massive mountains, but now they seemed to retreat faster than he could approach them.

He turned back to the ship and rubbed his eyes. The sun, already dipping low on its long glide to the horizon, lay behind her remaining masts, shining cold and bright. Concentric circles of light arced around the ship in a doubled halo, and frozen ice crystals drifted in the still air all about, like glittering diamonds in lazy flight. Joshua wondered wide-eyed at the stark beauty of it all, a smile stretching his chilled cheeks, till he began to cool down.

When he turned back ahead his smile vanished instantly. The clarity of the sky had gone, and an angry glower of cloud was surging down from the mountains and on to the ice. A moment more of watching showed it was moving fast, and straight towards him. As it came on, with terrifying speed, he made out a whirlwind of snow, sucked up from the surface and spinning like a giant top. 'A williwaw!' he gasped. He had been warned of these sudden furious winds, which roared down from the mountains, whipping up the snow into blinding blizzard, and tearing the very clothes from anyone caught outside.

He looked around frantically for any kind of shelter, and soon saw his only hope lay in a pressure ridge off to the east. A small berg stood frozen into the jumbled blocks, like the solitary oak in the hay meadow back home, where he'd sheltered from sudden thunderstorms. He turned and ran for it. There was no time to unharness the sledge, which bucked and hissed at his heels like an angry snake, while the gun and harpoon bounced painfully on his back.

He'd not gone a hundred yards when the williwaw hit. Wind shrieked around him, thick with snow which clogged his eyes and mouth and ears, so that he was running blind and deaf and unable to breathe. The wind forced him forward, stumbling wildly, until he fell full length, with a searing pain in his left ankle. The sledge slammed into him, cracking his head and knocking the air out of his chest. He struggled to his feet: but he could not walk, never mind run. And he knew he *had* to find shelter. Now.

He righted the upturned sledge, and clambered on to it, sitting upright with his arms outstretched, like the spars of his ship, to catch the driving wind. The sledge accelerated fast, and he dropped his hands to grip tightly as it bounced and scudded through the whiteout, heading who knew where.

It slammed into something and launched Joshua forward like a human snowball. He closed his eyes against the bone-crunching impact he knew would surely come, but, after an age in the air, he came to rest in soft snow piled against the pressure ridge.

He spluttered the snow from his face, and felt

blindly among the scattered ice-blocks for any hope of shelter from the howling wind. To his left was a kind of corner which offered some lee space. He hauled the sledge up, jammed it between two blocks of ice, and crawled underneath. He curled up as tight as he could, using his arms to shield a kind of breathing space around his face as the drifting snow rose all around.

When his panting had died down, and he knew he would not suffocate, he settled down to wait until the blizzard blew itself out, trying to shut himself off from the cold and the pain and the fear. He could do nothing else.

It was impossible to tell how long he had lain in the snow, for he could not say how far shivers stretch time. When the quiet came he did not know if it was due to a drop in the wind or a rise in the snow, but he did know he had to move on. He had drawn his hands up from his sleeves to wrap around his chest, but he could not protect his feet the same way, and now he could not feel them. At least that meant his turned ankle no longer hurt, when he kicked backwards, beneath his protective roof of sledge, at the wall of snow behind him. At first it felt as solid as the ice on either side, and a seed of panic sprouted in his chest at the thought of being trapped. He kicked on, and it began to give, so he kicked harder still, and soon was scrambling backwards out of his snowy burrow.

When at last he surfaced, and beat the snow out of his hair, he found the wind had died completely, and the air was as still as before – but the landscape around was transformed. He looked about, confused and uncertain, for his ship, or the mountains, but saw no sign of either. He looked up at the iceberg that towered above him. It had proved his protector from the blizzard, and now offered itself as a lookout tower.

He stamped and jumped, on ice-block feet, to try and bring some warmth back to his sluggish muscles, until he felt able to dig out the sledge. He unslung the gun, laid it on the sledge, and took the harpoon as a staff to help him clamber up the tumbled ice and on to the upper ramparts of the castellated berg. He looked round again, and still he recognised nothing, and knew he had to go higher. The iceberg sheered up another fifteen feet, and not a single foot-hold broke the smooth glaze of its surface.

'Where there's a will is a way,' he said, as he grasped the harpoon near its head and started scraping at the ice. Within minutes he had cut first one step at knee height, then another, level with his hip, and a third, up to his chest. He stepped back and slid his grip down the shaft, so he could raise the blade higher, to cut two more steps, one level with his head, and then the last, as high above it as he could reach. As soon as he had done he set to climbing, stabbing the harpoon into the ice and hauling himself up.

The work brought warmth to his body, and even some sweat, but as the blood ran back to his hands they tingled and burned. The higher he climbed the worse it got until, as he reached the summit of his little ice mountain, he was howling with the hurt of it. He sprawled on the flat top of the berg, until the fire in his hands died down. There was still no feeling at all in his feet, so he could only kneel, supported by his harpoon staff, as he surveyed the icy kingdom laid out below him.

It was as if he was seeing it for the first time, it looked so different. There were mountains, yes, but not where he expected them – and, strain his eyes though he might, he could see no ship. He guessed that by then the crew would have stripped her masts down and laid sails over the spars for their winter shelter. If on top there was now a wind-whipped dusting of snow, then she'd look no different from the many piled-up clumps of pressure ice that led in jagged lines from one horizon to another. Nor was the sun any help. In the middle of the day it hung in the southern sky, and at midnight it lay low in the north, but the difference was not great, and would not serve to navigate by unless he knew the time: and he did not.

All he had to go on was his inner sense of north, and here, on the top of the world, where poles multiplied and moved about, it had become confused. He shut his eyes to the sights around him and the shivers within, and tried to picture the compass needle inside his head. It was as if it swung behind a glass that was frosted by cold and fogged by pain, and he struggled to rub it clear. Soon he caught a glimmer of it, and concentrated harder still, till more glimpses came: once, twice, three times, a little longer and stronger each time, until they suddenly merged into the conviction he had known before. He spun to his right, shot out his arm and opened his eyes. 'There!' he croaked, in the shattered silence. And immediately the mountains he found himself pointing at *did* look familiar. He fixed in his view a particular peak as his needle of the north, and closed his eyes again, while he felt for where he now knew the *Aurora* would be, then turned to his left and pointed a second time. He did not expect to see his ship when he opened his eyes, but he knew she would be somewhere in the jumble of ice that trembled above his finger, and if he could only make his way there he would find her.

He clambered stiffly down, hitched the sledge to his harness, and set off, using the harpoon for a staff as he staggered on still-numb feet. At first he checked behind for his north-pointing mountain over and over, but each time he faced ahead again he felt a qualm of unease. For the first time since he'd left Whitby he had turned away from something that drew him irresistibly, something more than just a mark on a map or a point on a compass. Even though his life now depended on heading south to his ship, he felt a tug from the mountains and the pole beyond. It was as if he'd been struck by an invisible harpoon, and was being reeled in by King Neptune and his clan. They'd allow him to run south for a while, but they'd draw him on again: he knew it.

He whistled and sang to banish such thoughts, but gradually, as he grew colder and his fatigue deepened, he withdrew into a silent plodding world, where all that mattered was the next painful step, and the next, and then the next. When at intervals he forced himself to sing he could no longer remember the words, and his lips would not obey him long enough to hold a whistled note. He found himself humming the tune to 'From Greenland's Icy Mountains' over and over, if only to stop himself thinking about the cold.

Icy fingers clutched his chest and clawed at his cheeks, and slowly squeezed the feeling from his legs. He started to stumble, and then to fall, and his reactions were now so slow he crashed heavily to the ice each time. It was more and more of an effort to pick himself up, and every time he did he searched about in vain for his ship. After one such fall the gun dug into his ribs, and he cursed his cold-muddled thinking for not using it before. He knew he could not control his fingers to reload, so one shot was all he had. He unslung the weapon, aimed it at the sun, and squeezed the frozen trigger with a mittened hand and a silent prayer that he might be heard.

The sun fluttered to the horizon like a wounded bird, while thunderclaps echoed all around. Joshua was flung on his back by the force of the recoil, and pinned there by the depths of the silence which followed. There were no answering shots, no whistles, no shouts. Nothing.

He hurled the gun aside, but could not work the buckle to unharness the sledge, so he had to drag it with him still. He hauled himself to his knees and then what passed for his feet, and stumbled on. His shivering had stopped now, and a flicker of lovely warmth lit within him, growing steadily to fill his stomach like a feast of breakfast porridge. Something told him it was a trick, and he should not heed the wayward signals his frozen body sent him, but he lacked the will to resist the lulling warmth and ease. He slumped to the ice for what he knew would be the last time, for he had no strength to get up again. He lay back against the sledge and closed his eyes with a sigh.

He didn't have to walk, or work, any more that day. He'd been well fed and now rested by the fire, watching his father light up his pipe, and eager for his stories. He'd listen to the tales of the sea and the whaling, and wait to tell some stories of his own. Soon he'd be in his hammock, and the last thing he'd do before sleep would be to reach below and smooth the soft fur of loyal Nelson.

And here he came, his faithful dog: bounding over the hay meadow, full of yelps and vigour. He'd brought his friends, four or five of them, all barking now, and tugging hard at the strange long leads that tied them together. A little cart with no wheels slid along behind, and fur-clad figures hurried after it. Dog tongues lapped his face, in clouds of fish-fume breath, till weird words called them off. Broad-faced fur-men looked down on him, frowning. They spoke, but he could not hear them: they touched him, but he could feel nothing, and they stared at him, but he could no longer see. Everything was white and silent and still.

Chapter 22

Silence and stillness continued their reign when Joshua next came to: but white had been usurped. The darkness, unseen for months now, disorientated him, though he was sure he was awake, and neither dead nor delirious nor dreaming. He waited until his eyes accustomed to the little light that percolated through the ice-lined porthole, and then he looked around. He lay, swathed in blankets, in a bunk, in a cabin, in a ship. Blessed warmth coursed through him, though cold air nipped his exposed cheeks and he puffed clouds when he breathed. Something more than blankets swaddled his feet, more heavily on the left, where a nagging pain gnawed at his toes. Beyond this he had no idea where he was, or how he came to be there, or how long it had been.

He sat up, frowning, and tried to patch together brief and hazy pictures into a quilt of explanation. He remembered shooting the sun: perhaps that was why it was dark. He felt for the deck by his bunk, but knew he'd find no Nelson there, for his dog had come and gone, but at least he was not now alone. He had writhed in sweat-soaked bedding, while figures huddled at the end of his bunk, and the dull gnawing in his foot gave way to a searing fire. There had been visits, with whispered words, and flickering candles, and cool cloths laid on his brow. Between visits, there'd been a silent watcher he struggled to identify, reading by lamplight beside him. Sometimes he thought it was Bob Barrow, and at others Mr Colbeck, though mostly it had seemed to be the captain. But whenever Joshua tried to speak out, the figure always turned to him with the familiar face of his father, saying 'Shhhh!' and pulling the bedclothes higher, as he drifted back into sleep.

He'd seen the sun and the stars and most of the phases of the moon through the porthole by his pillow. He'd heard the shrieking winds all about, and footsteps overhead, and the creak of timbers below, and then, one still and sunny day, the shouts from a football match on the ice close by. That last one *must* have been a dream. He sighed and lay back, defeated, to stare at the ceiling. He needed more rest. It was so good to be warm.

The next time he awoke it was day, and he had company again. He still could not identify the burly figure by his bunk, but when the voice came he knew it at once as Bob Barrow's. 'All right lad?' he asked.

Joshua swung between delight and despondency. If it was Bob Barrow who spoke then he was not in the *Lindisfarne*. The faint hopes he harboured were snuffed out. 'Awake at last, eh?'

Joshua hadn't spoken for so long that his voice would not work. He nodded.

'Thought we'd lost you there. And in more ways than one. But you're a tough 'un, that's for sure. Here.' He handed Joshua a steaming mug of broth and a thick crust of breath. 'You must eat.'

Joshua let him talk, while he sipped the broth and nibbled at the bread. 'I'll never forget how you came back to the ship. We'd seen the williwaw from the masts and feared for your soul. Search parties went out where we thought you had gone, but returned empty-handed and quiet but for the cursing that we'd let you go hunting alone. One party said they thought they'd heard a shot, but the ice noise was so great that they couldn't be sure. Next thing we know there's a sledge racing up, dogs in front, Eskimo running after, and towing another, smaller, sledge. Yours.'

Joshua dropped his crust as a memory flashed up – the broad-faced fur-men!

'And there's a bundle under the fur. We think they've brought us seal-meat to trade, but they're shouting and waving, and they fling back the covers and it's you.' Another memory – wolf-fur over his face.

'And a right old state you're in. Half-dead with cold and frost-bit bad. We brought you straight up here to Mr Colbeck's cabin – he berths with me now, turn and turn about, hot-bunking like – and the whole crew stand watch to nurse you day and night. Even Edward Sumner – though he don't do Sundays, and there's been three o' them.'

Joshua's eyes widened. He'd been there three weeks?

Bob Barrow grinned. 'Aye, lad. That long. Even the Eskimo were worried about you. They've visited twice, travelling who knows how far, and mumbled over you and fed you potions.'

210

More memories; small people, dark-skinned, wide-faced, with smiling eyes, talking strangely and staring down at him. One, whose voice was higher than the rest, had hung something over his head. Joshua reached up to his throat to a necklace made of hide and strung with carved pieces of ivory. He felt along it for the clasp or at least a knot, till Bob Barrow stilled him. 'You're not to take that off, they said. Ever. It gave you back your life, but only works while you wear it.'

Joshua admired it, then suddenly let it drop and scrabbled around in a panicky search for what used to hang in its place, till Bob Barrow took his hand and slid it under his pillow, where it touched the cool brass of his compass. When he looked up, with a smile, he saw the leather case hanging from a nail by the porthole.

'No more scrapes for a while, lad. You've no room about your neck for any more charms.' He got up, and took the empty mug. 'And now that you've supped you should rest. We need your hunting skills before our stores run dry.'

The third time it was pain that woke him. Someone was unwrapping his left foot and it hurt. He cried out, surprising Mr Colbeck and Donald Lewis, who turned to him sharply, and closed up, so he could not see what they were at.

'Sorry, Joshua, but we must redress it,' said Colbeck.

'Redress what?' he croaked. They were the first words he had said in a month but they met with no reply. 'Redress what?' he demanded, when the pain bit again.

Colbeck and Lewis looked at each other then moved apart. 'This.'

Joshua gasped. His foot was a misshapen multi-coloured mess, swollen and blackened and cracked. Green stuff oozed out from fissures in the skin. He counted, over and over, but never got past three. Two of his toes, the smallest ones, had gone.

'It looks bad, I know son, but believe me it's getting better. Time was we thought you'd lose your leg.'

'Will . . . w-w-w-will I walk?'

Mr Colbeck looked at Donald Lewis. 'Fetch the cooper,' he said. Some minutes later old Benjamin Watt stepped into the cabin. Joshua hardly knew him, as he didn't keep watch nor clamber in the rigging with the rest. He was fully employed below decks making and repairing the barrels in which the ship stored her precious cargo.

After a mumbled conversation in the doorway, old Benjamin stooped and undid his right boot. Joshua stared, spellbound. When the thick woollen sock came off the cooper stood before him on something that was more a pad than a foot, for it bore not a single toe. He paced up and down the cabin, with the merest trace of a limp. 'Do I not walk?' he asked Joshua, who could do nothing but nod. 'And can I not stand?' He balanced on his toeless pad, while waving his other leg about. 'Did you know? Could you tell?' Joshua shook his head.

''Tis one of the costs of becoming a polar man, my lad,' said Mr Colbeck. 'You have paid your fee early, though all of us pay in the end. You will walk, and run, and climb, but when you look at your foot you will know where you have been. And how it nearly ended.'

Benjamin slipped his sock back on, and bent to secure his boot. He winked at Joshua. 'Tell you what, lad,' he wheezed, with a conspiratorial grin. 'Come back next year and I'll show you the other one.' He cackled, Mr Colbeck and Donald Lewis stifled sniggers, and an answering laugh rose within Joshua, despite the hurt and the horror of what he had seen. It spilled out, to mingle with the laughter of his crewmates, and rattle round the cabin, and light the smiles of all aboard who heard it.

*

The cabin door swung open, and Bob Barrow and Benjamin Watt stepped in, swirled in clouds of their own breath. 'Come on, lad,' one said, as he pulled back Joshua's heavy bedding. 'It's time you were up.' Cold air clamped down on Joshua's chest, to trigger instant shivers. He looked about in vain for his stock of heavy sweaters, but Bob Barrow held out instead a garment of thick but surprisingly light fur. 'The Eskimo left you this. An *anorak* they called it.'

Joshua slipped it over his head and slid his arms into the wide sleeves. It was made of sealhide, lined with soft fur, and carried a deep hood, which was fringed with even thicker, softer fur, the warmest he had ever felt. His shivers soon stopped. He swung his legs out of the bed and struggled to get into his now-tattered overtrousers. Bob Barrow handed him one sea-boot – the right – but when Joshua reached out for the other he shook his head. 'No weight on that foot yet a-while,' he said. 'So you won't need no boot.'

Benjamin Watt handed him two crutches he had obviously just made. 'Here, son. We measured you up while you was sleepin'. Let's see if we got it right, eh?' Joshua wobbled upright on his good foot, supported by a sailor on either side, until he slipped a crutch under each armpit.

They were exactly the right size. 'Steps will be tricky, so just take your time, eh?' Bob Barrow called after him as he shot out of the door and up on to the deck.

The winter shelter covered most of the ship apart from the raised sections at bow and stern, and the deck was cluttered with stowed spars and other gear, but Joshua had soon marked out a circuit. Once his eyes had accustomed to the glare, and his shrivelled muscles to movement, he set off bump-swinging his way round and round. First ten times clockwise, then ten the other way, then rest and repeat.

He was unsteady, at least at first, blisters soon bubbled under his mittens, and his armpits hurt where the crutches dug in, but he hardly noticed he was so delighted to be outside and mobile. His speed increased, but his cornering skills did not keep pace, and on his twenty-ninth lap he bumped into Mr Colbeck, nearly knocking him over. It was all Joshua could do to stay upright himself, and he looked up, in fear of a scolding. Colbeck stared down with a pained expression and rubbed his ribs. 'Right, lad. Now that you're driving us all mad, what with your bumping round the deck above our heads, and knocking us aside like nine-pins, I'd say it's time I had my bunk back.'

Joshua collected his belongings from Colbeck's cabin, and returned on deck, shuffling up the steps on his backside and dragging his meagre bundle and his crutches after him. He paused by the fo'c'sle door, listening, then pulled his hood up, pushed the door open with his crutch, and stepped inside. A sudden silence fell. Donald Lewis was the first to speak. "Ey-up, boys,' he said, 'Eskimo moving in.' A gruff welcome rumbled round the cramped and smoky cabin.

It was ended, inevitably, by Edward Sumner. 'Just so long as 'e don't bring no 'eathen 'abits,' he grumbled.

'And especially no Eskimo food,' retorted Nathaniel Bridge. His shipmates returned to their cards, while Joshua rigged his hammock above them once more, stifling a smile.

Chapter 23

Joshua's daily exercise on deck built up a huge appetite, and the vast platefuls of food he downed at dinner fuelled a speedy recovery, so that he was soon touching down with the two remaining toes on his left foot, and adapting his boot as best he could. Each morning he was eager to be out and active, even though the darkness lingered longer every day, and soon he found himself up before the sun. One such half-lit dawn saw the ship coated in ice-rime, a frosting of ice that covered the deck and all the remaining rigging, and made it look like a ghost ship, however solid it was to the touch. Joshua flipped up his hood and waited for the sun.

When it arrived, roused by the smells of breakfast from the galley, the light it cast was playing strange tricks again. Upside down mountains hovered in the air, dissolving and reforming even as he watched. He held out his hand, as if to touch them. Distant peaks danced on his palm to the hiss of frying bacon.

Joshua frowned. The bacon had run out months ago, and the cook never fried anything. He listened, frozen with held-out hand, and gasped at the tiny specks that slid from finger-tip to finger-tip, as if leaping great chasms. It was an utterly windless day, the kind where sound carried impossibly far, and soon, added above the hiss, he heard the yips and yelps of distant dogs. At intervals came other sounds – *ili*, *iu* – foreign to his ear but unmistakably human voices. And all the while the specks grew larger, and separated into dogs, and sleds, and people wearing fur. The *Aurora* had visitors.

Joshua snapped his hand to his side as he turned to the hatchway behind him. 'Eskimo!' he shouted. 'The Eskimo are coming!' There was increased urgency in the bleary stirring within, while, from another hatch near the stern, emerged the captain, who had clearly been awake some time. Joshua pointed at the approaching specks. The captain screwed up his

218

eyes and stared where Joshua was indicating, then smiled back at him. 'Glad to see your eyesight's no worse for your escapade, young Murphy,' he said.

The crew gathered one by one on deck, yawning and stretching themselves awake as the two sleds approached. A short way off, another shouted command drew the dogs to a reluctant halt. They stood in harness, panting, for a time, then curled up on the ice, tails over their muzzles, while their masters busied themselves unloading bundles. One man stayed with the sled while four others walked across to the gangplank. They clambered up it and set down their burdens on deck, to be greeted warmly by captain and crew.

Joshua stared at the visitors and their clothes. They wore anoraks, just like his own, but with more decoration, as well as trousers of the same design and large fur boots and mittens. None of them were tall, but one was smaller than the rest, and of a height with Joshua. Joshua and the boy both hung back while the men exchanged welcomes and began their barter.

Joshua listened to their strange language: a rich mixture of clicking *q*s and *k*s, hissing *s*s and lilting *l*s, and sonorant *m*s and *n*s. The captain seemed to understand most of what they said, and even spoke some words back, though the rest of the crew conversed in gestures and pointings and nods. When one such gesture was directed at Joshua, the Eskimo turned to him together and smiled. One of them, who had done most of the talking, drew the boy forward, and laid a proud hand on his shoulders. The captain translated when he spoke. 'Compass Murphy: meet Simva, who heard your signal shot and spied you from afar.'

Joshua stared as Simva was pushed shyly towards him. He held out his hand, but Simva ignored it, raising his own hands to lower first Joshua's hood and then his own. Joshua took in the smooth red-brown skin, the brilliant teeth, the seal-like eyes, and the silken masses of hair, dark as Whitby jet, that spilled down; and gasped when he realised what it meant – he owed his life to a girl.

Simva stepped closer still, her face approaching his. Panic churned within his chest. She was going to kiss him! He'd not been kissed for half his lifetime, and now it was going to happen here, in front of his crewmates, and there was not a thing he could do to stop her. Joshua's panic peaked as her smiling face filled his gaze, and then receded, with huge relief, when the only contact that came was a brief rub of noses.

Hers was warm, his cold. He released a long-held breath when she stepped back, but, just as he relaxed, his left hand crutch skidded away from him on the ice-slick deck, and he went sprawling backwards to bang his head on the capstan.

He lay there, writhing in an agony of embarrassment, and pretending that the pain was only physical, as the laughter rang around him. The Eskimo leader laughed loudest, and spoke to Simva in tones of pride. Joshua picked out, as well as her name, a word – *pitiraq* – which made her and the others laugh again.

He struggled to his feet – to his foot – then turned away from the crowd, to hide his blushes, and disappeared below without a word. The barter carried on without him: fur boots for an axe, seal-meat for a mirror, bear-hide for a knife. No one noticed the rat-a-tat hammering from the cooper's workshop below.

The visitors were making ready to leave when Joshua emerged once more. He set off on his familiar bump-swing circuit, faster than ever before. After one lap he sped towards the crowd, came to an abrupt halt with a half-turn flourish, and planted his crutches into the ice-laden deck with a satisfying crunch and a look of triumph.

Hearing this, the captain reached across and took a crutch from him. Joshua balanced carefully while the crutch was displayed so that all could see the nails Joshua had driven into the base to give him some grip on the ice. All the visitors admired the implement. Joshua knew that wood and metal were rarities in their world. What impressed them most was the casual ease with which a mere boy could hammer precious nails into even more precious wood with not a word of censure. The leader patted Joshua on his his head. '*Ningaq*!' he said, with a grin.

Joshua turned to his captain for translation. 'His daughter blew you over just as the williwaw – the *pitiraq* – did: but you have *ningaq*, fighting spirit. He likes that.'

Joshua blushed again, but with pride this time. There was more talk between Simva's father and the captain, who turned to him, impressed. 'He wants you to visit his camp.'

Before Joshua could reply Simva stepped forward and spoke to her father in a rapid babble. Two words emerged repeatedly – Eskimo and something that sounded like *inn-wit*. Simva's father nodded while the captain translated once more. 'Simva says you can only come if you never again speak of Eskimo. She heard you shout it across the ice but it is a term they do not value. They call themselves *Inuit*. It means "the people" and comes from a time when they counted themselves the only inhabitants of Earth.'

Joshua looked directly at Simva and held out his hand once more. This time she did not ignore it, nor threaten him with a kiss. As they shook he gestured towards her and her kin, with a bow to indicate apology and understanding. 'Inuit,' he said. Then he straightened, a twinkle in his eye, and indicated his crewmates: 'Yorkshire.'

'Iuksir,' she repeated, smiling.

Joshua laughed out loud at the joy of it. He sat atop an Inuit sledge, ecstatic at the speed with which the dogs drew it on. When the ice was flat and the going good, Simva sat in front of him, and her father behind. When the ice was broken, and progress slower, they walked or ran alongside, Simva's father shouting directions to the dogs, who never faltered in their response. Joshua soon learnt, as had the dogs long before him, that *ili* meant right and *iu* left, and practised, under his breath, when he had the sledge to himself.

The second sledge followed far behind, and much more slowly, accompanied as it was by a troop of trudging sailors and their own clumsy carts. Joshua was almost glad that the loss of his toes had given him this privilege. The sledge itself, which he had inspected closely as the dogs were hitched and his crutches lashed down, astounded him. Its runners were made of frozen fish, lapped head to tail and wrapped in seal hide, and coated with a careful moulding of fresh water ice and moss. They were lashed by caribou-hide thongs to a framework of walrus bone, across which was laid a platform of hide. The whole thing was fast and light, and flexed beneath him as it ran over irregular ice. It was also almost entirely edible: Joshua wondered if times ever got that bad.

The Inuit camp was closer than he thought. Four or five large tents clustered in the lee of a rocky outcrop, just off the sea-ice. Joshua swung off the sledge, aware that, for the first time since Orkney months before, there was land beneath his feet, crusted though it was in ice utterly indistinguishable from that which imprisoned him and his ship. Dogs and children scampered up in a chorus of barking and shrieks, which rose to a peak and fell away as Joshua was escorted to the middle tent.

The entrance was low, and covered by a flap of hide held down by stones. Joshua crawled through, behind Simva and her father. He peered about in the dim light from a blubber lamp and a translucent seal-gut window panel.

At the further, wider, end of the tent were several raised platforms, covered in moss and thick furs, which he guessed to be the sleeping-places. To one side, near the blubber lamp, an elderly couple sat, motionless and watchful. Joshua was presented to them while still on his knees. The old woman got to her feet, and bowed unsteadily before tending the cooking implements by the lamp. The old man did not rise. There was much Inuit chatter. Joshua listened closely, and picked out one or two words he was coming to know, such as *kabloonah*, which meant white man. Whenever Simva used it, she linked it with another word – *iuksir* – and a wink at Joshua.

Joshua watched the old lady at work, and saw again how nearly everything the Inuit used came from the animals they hunted. The tent was made of hide, on a whalebone framework; blubber gave heat and light; caribou and musk-ox pelts served as blankets. Bowls and plates were made of whalebone, spoons and knives of walrus ivory, and drinking cups fashioned from musk-ox horns. Joshua was handed one, brimful of a foaming liquid he was meant to drink. He gulped at it and passed it on, still unsure of its contents.

It took him some time to see how keenly the

old man eyed his crutches. Joshua handed them over for him to inspect, but instead the old man rose with a huge toothless grin to balance upon them. Only as he made off out of the tent did Joshua see that his right leg ended just below the knee. Joshua heard him cackling wildly as he careered around outside, to the laughter of the children and the barking of the dogs.

Joshua turned to Simva for explanation. '*Nanook*,' she said. He frowned. Without warning she pounced on him, her claw-like hands held high, a deep roar in her throat, and a hideous scowl on her face. Joshua jumped back, but just as quickly she returned to her serene and smiling self. '*Nanook*,' she repeated quietly, and only then did Joshua understand that the old man had lost his leg to the white bear.

The old lady, who had pretended not to notice how easily he startled, pointed to his foot. '*Nanook*?' she wheezed.

Joshua shook his head. '*Pitiraq*!' he said, as if he were a native.

Simva smiled, despite herself. '*Ajaqnak*.' She and the old lady shrugged together. He'd have to ask the captain later what it meant.

Another round of barking heralded the arrival of the second sledge with its escort of *Aurora* crew. There were greetings, and more barter, but all the pointings and gestures were soon stilled by an epic feast of Inuit food, which even Nathaniel Bridge ate until he was bursting. When they emerged, hours later, swollen-bellied and groaning, for the trip back to the ship, the long twilight had begun.

Joshua was loaded on to a sledge as before, but this time with only one crutch, and the sledge he rode was his own, hauled by his sailor mates as if he were an Egyptian king. He felt dozy from the food, and warmed by his furs, but mostly his toasty glow came from the way the old man, and behind him Simva, had looked at him when he handed over one of his crutches on leaving.

The way back was marked by an arch-shaped iceberg, frozen into the pack ice. On the right it was lit by the rosy rays of the dying sun, and, on the left, gilded gold and silver by the alloy light of the rising moon. Different coloured shadows crossed in front of it, and the purple-grey dark in the archway beneath was almost luminous too. It lay off their path, but although no order was given, their tracks bent towards it irresistibly, and the little group passed under the arch, all staring upwards in silent wonder at the cathedral splendour overhead. No one spoke until back aboard ship.

In the fo'c'sle that night Joshua listened as his shipmates swung lazily in their hammocks, bloated and belching and snoring loudly, as if the spirits of all the seals and walrus they had eaten had returned to inhabit their beached and sleeping bodies.

Chapter 24

Joshua was hunting again as soon as he could, but now in the Inuit way, tutored by Simva and her father. Joshua was glad to have a father at hand, even if he was not his own, and shared no language with him. They sat together for long silent hours by the breathing holes, harpoon in hand, willing a seal to the surface, and calmly waiting for the surge, the rush of bubbles, and then the sudden burst with which they came. A single well-timed strike could secure food for a day, heat and light for a week, and clothing for a season. Simva explained in mime that unless her father intoned an Inuit prayer, and thanked the seal for giving up its life to provide him and his people with their means of survival, then other seals would come no more. Joshua tried in turn to put questions about the *Lindisfarne*, but could not make himself understood, and was so frustrated by her bafflement that he had to stop.

He was taken to the hunting holes by sledge, and often invited to try his hand at driving the dogs. But he was used to a single dog, who never questioned his authority, and they were used to sharp commands in an accentless Inuit tongue, so that he never mastered it. Time after time he ended up with the dogs in a snarling tangle, the sledge on its side, and himself tipped on to the ice. He began to think they did it deliberately, as if to mock him. Once, the dogs saw a seal before he did and took off towards it, heedless of his pleas to stop. He was bucked off the sledge but not flung free, and found himself dragged over bone-hard and tooth-sharp ice by tangled traces.

The dogs only stopped at the seals' hole, where of course the seal itself was long gone. Joshua lay at the edge of the smoking water, battered, cut and bruised, struggling to get his breath back and untangle his feet. When the dogs stopped barking at the seal, and then at each other, they turned to look down at him. Only now, from below, did Joshua clearly see the way their mouths turned up at the corners, in a permanent superior smile which made him angry. He was used to people laughing at him: it happened all the time in Whitby. But not animals, and not here, and not in front of Simva.

She rushed up, torn between concern and hilarity, to untangle the dogs and her *iuksir*-boy. '*Ajaqnak*!' she laughed at him, but he still didn't know what it meant, and was in no mood to listen. She was dismayed to see his face contorted with pent-up anger as he scrabbled to his knees. All the hot fury he felt for Laurence and Flint and Hestall and Wisely, which he'd carried around deep within, now found a vent and burst through his thick crust of control in an eruption of outrage.

He curled his hand into a fist and punched the nearest smirking dog. His mitten, and beneath it his knuckles, ripped open on the dog's sharp teeth. The dog yelped in surprise and pain, then cowered at his feet, as the blood of dog and boy mingled on the ice. The other dogs shrank back in their traces, eyes fixed upon him. Simva, who could command these beasts with a whisper, watched too.

Joshua knelt before the first dog, grasped the loose fur on either side of its neck, and forced it to meet his fierce gaze, which he held until there was no doubt who was master. He released the animal, which stood with its tail between its legs, and moved forward to the next, and then the next, repeating the ritual.

When he reached the lead dog, a big ice-hardened hound, he knew he faced a challenge. It stared back at him through impassive sky-blue eyes, subtly baring just the tips of its teeth. Joshua drew his face closer while Simva winced. She knew this dog and its history: her father hadn't made it leader for nothing.

Joshua approached closer yet, till his nose almost met its muzzle. Still it stared back, lips twitching. Joshua knew that a single snap could tear his throat open and spill on to the ice all the blood in his body, and not just the thin dribble from his torn knuckles. But he also knew he could not – he would not – back down. The moment stretched out. All the other dogs made themselves small and Simva stood utterly still. The wind stopped.

A drop of saliva fell from the dog's teeth, half-frozen before it hit the ice. There was a flicker of hesitation in the dog's defiance – and Joshua sprang. He snapped to his feet with a fearsome roar, blood-stained hands spread high beside his face, and scowling hideously. The dog flinched and ducked as Joshua's roaring echoed back from distant mountains; and then, in the silence which followed, he heard the whimper and saw the cower which told him he had won. He didn't hear Simva begin to breathe again.

Never again did the dogs defy him, or race ahead out of control, or try to buck him off. He was even able to race them against Simva's team, when they took separate sledges, not minding that she always won, because he was almost able to match her haul of seals.

A breathless snow-spray turn brought his sledge to a halt just behind Simva's, at the edge of her family's camp. Her cousins and kin were engaged in cutting blocks of compacted snow from the lee of the nearby rocks. She turned to him, a wide smile upon her face. '*Iklu*!' she beamed, as she jumped from her sledge to unleash her dogs and join in. Joshua took his time with his own team, giving each dog a pat and a word, even if they did not understand the language. He reserved extra warmth for the dog he had hit. All of them looked at him different-ly now.

Simva's grandfather stood aside, proudly balanced on his single crutch. Joshua joined him. Their sound legs – Joshua's right, the old man's left – pressed together for stability. It felt like lining up for some strange three-legged race.

233

They watched as a perfect ring of snowblocks was laid upon the ice. Simva stepped over them into the centre and gestured him forward. Joshua hesitated until the old man pushed him onward with his crutch and a cackle. He knelt beside Simva, as her aunts and uncles and cousins laid more rings of blocks upon the first, and watched as she helped secure them in place. Simva's father drew up with a block of clear fresh-water ice on his sledge. He and two others carefully positioned it in the rising rows of rings, as a window.

As the rings rose they tilted inwards, fitting together as neatly as any course of stones in a Whitby home. Simva supported them as they tilted ever further to close overhead in an icy dome, until all but a fist-sized gap was left directly above. She giggled as Joshua looked anxiously around. The two of them were completely enclosed in a hemisphere of ice, cut off from the world outside, though they could see shadows through their makeshift window, and hear laughter through the aperture above.

Simva waited, apparently enjoying his discomfort, before producing a long pointed bone knife. She narrowed her eyes and turned slowly round, as if testing for the intensity of the dying sun's light, just he had spun for his north. She stopped and pointed in the direction Joshua immediately knew was south-east, then knelt, and dug her knife into the new-laid snow-blocks, patiently cutting a U-shaped entrance from the floor to somewhere above knee height.

The blocks she cut were pulled away from the outside, and Simva crawled through, waving Joshua to follow. He emerged to a smiling circle of Inuit igloo-builders, already bearing more blocks to fashion the entrance passage of their new winter home. Joshua stood back in admiration as the igloo was completed, the joins between the blocks packed with loose snow, and the contents of the nearest tent moved in, piece by piece. When he was invited in once more he was amazed at how homely and how warm the two-hour old ice-house already was.

Joshua's strength waxed as the daylight waned, so that just as the sun bade a final farewell for the winter he cast aside his remaining crutch to walk unaided, if limping. He was now able to go hunting alone. His shipmates increasingly came to rely on the supplies of seal-meat he brought in, and did not object that he spent more and more time in the Inuit camp. Every time he returned he had acquired another item of Inuit clothing or hunting gear. The piece he treasured most was a snow glare mask, made of stiffened hide, fringed with ivory to keep its shape. It bore a single horizontal slit, criss-crossed by two small vertical cuts, one for each eye. He slung it round his neck even on days he knew he would not need it, and loved to put it on just before he returned to the ship.

Once he got Simva to wear her own mask and enter the fo'c'sle in place of him. He listened outside as the sailors offered up their gruff greetings. 'All right, lad?' they asked, not expecting a reply because Joshua rarely gave one. When he was sure Simva's struggle to get into the unfamiliar hammock was done, he put on his own mask and knocked on the door. Nathaniel Bridge stomped up and opened it. He stood on the threshold, frowning in mystified silence. 'No thanks,' he said, eventually. 'We've already got one half-Eskimo boy.'

Joshua removed his mask. 'Oh no you haven't,' he said, as a girlish giggle bubbled up from his hammock and Simva's laughing face looked over the edge. A broad grin spread across Bridge's weather-beaten face as he looked from one to the other, and knew that he and his crew-mates had been completely taken in. He looked at Joshua. ' 'Ave you tried that in t' Eskimo camp yet?'

Joshua shook his head. There was something he had to do before his next visit there. Before Simva said her farewells, he sought out Benjamin Watt. They had worked together most of the morning at Watt's bench, re-fashioning the stem of Joshua's now-redundant crutch into a peg-leg, with a leather cup for a stump, and hide thongs to secure it in place. Joshua did not want to embarrass the old man by giving it to him directly, so he asked Simva to take it back with her. She ran her hands over it with grateful delight, then bundled it up and lashed it carefully to her sledge, knowing it was a rare treasure. She waved to Joshua as she sped off into a twilight deepened by gathering storm clouds.

Chapter 25

Although it was the middle of the day the darkness was total. A blizzard swirled thickly outside, obscuring stars and moon, as it had for days now. All the hatches were battened down and the crew only went above if absolutely necessary. No one left the ship, for they would be lost within yards and frozen within minutes. Storms like this had been frequent and prolonged, but this was the worst of the winter so far.

The captain had done what he could to inspire his men in the morning's service but he had failed to banish the air of sullen torpor that hung over his crew. Now he sat at his desk and pondered what he could say to them in the evening service to come, while the men swung listlessly in their fo'c'sle hammocks, tootling on the penny whistle, playing cards, and trying to ignore Edward Sumner.

At the large table in the captain's cabin Joshua sat in his anorak and mittens, surrounded by navigation tables and heavy texts. Long words and endless numbers swirled across the pages like the inky blizzard outside, disorientating him.

'Sir?' he ventured. The candle at his elbow flickered in the icy draught. 'Sir?'

'Mmmm?'

'What does *ajaqnak* mean? The Inuit say it a lot. Usually about me.'

'Oh?' The captain stared out of the porthole, a look of concentration on his face, then turned to him. 'We have no single word for it. So it goes, or such is life, or a shrug of the shoulders catch its meaning best. It is said when things go wrong.'

'That fits.' Joshua hoped not to hear it again, and both resumed their scratching, Joshua at his navigation exercises and the captain at his sermon.

'And *ilira*? Simva says it of the icebergs, and the mountains, and once of a whale.'

The captain smiled. 'I fear you lack concentration, lad. But no matter: some interruptions I welcome. Again we have no single word. Think of it as dangerous beauty, or beautiful danger. Something like that.'

Again they resumed their scratching, but this time the captain was waiting for another question. He didn't expect the one that came. 'Did my father ever learn their tongue?'

The captain set down his quill. 'No. He did not. But he did not have your need or opportunity. We hardly saw the Inuit on our two seasons together, and we were fully engaged on our whaling. What a hunter he was.' There was a long pause. One of the candles flickered out. 'As, I trust, he still is.'

'Will you teach me the words I need to ask the Inuit about other ships?'

'That I will.' The captain didn't tell Joshua it was futile, for these were among the first questions he had put to Simva's father months before, and he knew what the answer would be. But it was important to keep the boy busy, to keep his quest alive. He looked down at his much-crossed out sermon, then crumpled up the paper. And if it was important for Joshua to have a purpose, then why not the rest of them? He stood up abruptly.

'Compass Murphy!'

'Sir?'

'Summon the crew.'

Minutes later Joshua huddled in the freezing hold with the rest of the men. Grumbles and muttering rose around him, only quelled when the captain stood before them.

'Gentlemen. Four days hence 'tis midwinter's day, and Christmas follows after.' He paused, looking from man to man. 'We shall soon be closer to the spring that is yet to come, and will release us, than the autumn that is gone and which consigned us to this cold dark place.' He paused again, knowing he had their attention now. 'So let there be a feast!' The murmuring resumed, but in a different tone. 'And in the spirit of the day, we shall entertain the Inuit, in repayment of their hospitality.' Heads nodded all around, especially Joshua's. 'There will be no service now, for we must get to work. You may sing, if you wish, as you go about it.'

The crew dispersed in a healthy hubbub, to the galley and the stores, and soon a spontaneous chorus of 'In the Bleak Midwinter' rang around the ship, followed by laughter when they forgot the words and only Edward Sumner's croaky voice ran on.

The blizzard lifted overnight, and a full moon lit their way as Joshua and Mr Hobbs set off across the ice for the Inuit camp, Mr Hobbs bearing an invitation, and Joshua rehearsing his string of questions. Before he could put them, before he even reached the tents and igloos, he was assailed on all sides by Inuit, old and young; all limping, pointing to perfectly healthy legs, and miming amputations and their wish for wooden legs they could call their own. Joshua knew that wood was precious, there being no trees for thousands of miles: but he did not think until then it could be more precious than flesh.

When he had made it clear he would only make wooden legs for those who lacked a real one, he sought out first the old man in his igloo. If anyone could tell him, he would. The blubber lamp flame flickered more brightly in the old man's eyes at Joshua's entrance, and he promptly stood up. He patted his wooden leg, now polished to a high sheen, and demonstrated how well he walked upon it, with a huge grin on his face, till he saw that Joshua had come for something more than thanks. Joshua waited till he had sat down once more before he put the questions he had practised, over and over, since his last lesson in the captain's cabin.

Had he seen or heard any hint of another *kabloonah* ship, stuck like his a year before? The reply was the same as that which later came from every other Inuit he asked: a shrug of the shoulders and a shake of the head. In years gone by, yes. But not last year. Not here. No.

Chapter 26

There was just enough room in the captain's cabin for the crew and the visiting Inuit, although not all could sit at the table. Only Edward Sumner was absent, wallowing in gloomy solitude in the fo'c'sle. The captain had conducted a stark and simple service before the Inuit arrived; but it was not enough to soothe Sumner's religious fervour, or quell his bitter protests about sharing his Christmas dinner with the heathen, and on a Sunday too.

Joshua and Simva sat cross-legged on the floor, as out of the way as they could get. Joshua watched her wonder at the woody cavern where they gathered. The great oak beams and panels shone lustrously in the light from the candles and oil lamps, and none more so than the massive table, now groaning under the weight of the banquet and the pewter mugs of beer laid out upon it.

The cook had worked double watches since the feast was announced, though Nathaniel Bridge said it was only to warm himself the longer at the galley stove. His work, and the secret supplies the captain had held back for just such a purpose, combined to make a memorable meal, now topped off by the great chunks of walrus steak Simva's father unwrapped. At the very centre of the table was a huge and steaming Christmas pudding, decorated with the remnants of the Mayday garland. Joshua thought back to last year, when there had been no pudding at the Flint farmhouse.

When the visitors and crew were seated at last, the captain called silence and said grace. Simva frowned a question at Joshua, who explained, as best he could, that the captain was thanking the Christmas pudding for giving up its life to sustain them. Simva nodded solemnly, not noticing the gleam in his eye or the giggle he suppressed, at least until Bob Barrow, who had overheard, turned from the table.

'And just how, Master Murphy, do you catch

a Christmas pudding?' he rasped, in the silence which lingered yet after grace.

Joshua was mortified. Everyone's eyes turned to him, his private joke laid bare like a gutted fish. His eyes popped and his mouth opened and closed but no words came out. He was floundering: but he had to say something.

'You wait till a market day in October and you hide by the bank with a net. They're hungry for money but only ever eat farthings.'

The gathered throng looked at Joshua, then at each other, and then at Joshua again. Silence stretched. Nathaniel Bridge was the first to laugh, but the others soon caught on, including the Inuit, although they did not know what they were laughing at.

When the uproar died down all the formal stiffness of the occasion had gone, and then began a truly memorable meal. Course followed course, washed down by beer, till even the Inuit groaned and rubbed their swollen bellies. When not interrupted by eating, conversation and laughter grew steadily in volume and raucousness, until at last the captain decided it was pudding time.

He stood up slowly, then took a ceremonial sword from its hangings above the window, and laid it on the table, still in its scabbard. He removed the Mayday garlands from the pudding and passed them to left and right. Donald Lewis immediately put one on his head. The Inuit laughed at this, but their laughter was cut off short by a unified gasp as the sword was unsheathed. They had never seen so much metal, so shiny, and so sharp.

'*Ilira*!' said Joshua proudly.

Simva and her father turned to him together, obviously impressed by his expanding vocabulary. '*Ilira*!' they chorused in reply.

The captain raised the sword before him with both hands, then muttered something in a strange accent. All Joshua could make out was '. . . great chieftain o' the pudding race . . .' before the sword fell with a flourish, rapidly carving large chunks of pudding, which steamed afresh where they had been sliced.

On his third slice there was a loud clink as the sword struck metal. Once again all eyes turned to Joshua. 'Perhaps he's right!' said the captain. He pushed the slices apart with his sword and wafted the steam aside.

'A shilling if it's a farthing!' Bob Barrow called out.

'And half a crown for a penny!' replied Nathaniel Bridge.

Both men stood up and reached across the

table to shake hands. 'Done!' they said, as the captain laid his sword aside and rummaged in the crumbling chunks with his fingers. He pulled out a dull bronze coin, wiped it clean, and passed it to Joshua, who held it up for all to see. "Tis a farthing, sir.'

'Then take it as a token, Compass Murphy,' declared the captain. 'You came on board unbidden, with nothing but a compass and a quest. And now you are a navigator with a nose for north, and you hunt and dress and speak like an Inuit.' He paused. Joshua did not know where to look. Simva took his hand as the captain resumed: 'Perhaps you are becoming one and we should leave you here.'

'Amen to that,' muttered Nathaniel Bridge. 'I can't afford to lose no more wagers.'

When the laughter died down the captain continued. 'What you have lost in toes you have more than made up in skills with which to make your way in the world.' He raised his glass. 'Well done, sir!'

Everybody cheered, even Nathaniel Bridge, and in the hubbub no one noticed Joshua pass the coin to Simva, who turned it over and over in her hand and rubbed it till it shone.

Mr Colbeck made as if to distribute the pudding chunks, till the captain stilled his hand.

'Another ingredient yet,' he said smiling, as he turned to his cabinet and pulled out a bottle of brandy. He opened it and glugged half its contents over the pile of pudding pieces. A powerful smell filled the room, prompting Simva's father to dip a finger in and taste it. His face dissolved in grimaces and spluttering.

'The lights, gentlemen, if you would.' Candles were snuffed and the oil lamps turned down, till the cabin was almost as dark as the barren icescape outside. There was an expectant hush, extended by the captain until he was sure he had everyone's attention. He struck a match and lit the brandy. Gently dancing blue flames fluttered over the platter, flecked with yellow and green and orange. Murmurs of delight rippled round the table. Simva laughed out loud at the beauty.

'Your plates, gentlemen,' said the captain. He looked at Simva, as if seeing her for the first time. 'And lady,' he said, with a little bow. He dished out the pudding pieces while they were still alight. Flaming platefuls were passed around the table and handed down to Joshua and Simva on the floor. A few drops of burning brandy fell to the timbers between them, flickered a farewell, and went out.

The cabin, now dark again, filled with the clink of spoons upon plates. Joshua, who had been saving himself for this, finished first, and looked up, hopeful for more. His gaze was taken by more blue-green flickers, but this time through the window, behind the captain's head. Someone was serving pudding outside.

He gripped Simva's arm and pointed. She wiped the crumbs from her lips and nodded, but did not seem at all surprised. The captain turned to follow Joshua's pointing finger and saw it too. He turned back to the table. 'And now your mugs, gentlemen.' He sloshed a little brandy into each, and bade them all stand for a toast. A chorus of chairs scraped back.

The captain held his brandy mug before him in one hand, and with the other made a sweeping gesture which took in, at one and the same time, the wooden walls of the cabin and the display in the sky outside it. 'The *Aurora*!' he said. Everyone toasted along with him, and settled back into their chairs amid much coughing and spluttering, especially from the Inuit.

'But what is it?' asked Joshua, of no one in particular. He was the only one, apart from Donald Lewis, who had not seen it before.

'T' northern lights, lad,' said Mr Hobbs.

'The Merry Dancers, they call it in Orkney,' said Mr Colbeck.

'Aurora Barry Always, in Edinburgh,' said

Bob Barrow. 'Some kind o' 'eavenly firework display.'

'And Lord knows what they call it up 'ere,' said Nathaniel Bridge.

Joshua rummaged in the corner for his anorak and mittens. 'Permission to go above sir?' he asked. Whatever they called it he wanted to see it properly.

The captain smiled. 'Of course, lad. Just don't come down frostbit. And see if you can hear it whisper.'

Joshua clambered up the captain's companionway steps, with Simva close behind, and emerged to a world of wonder. Below, the renewed blaze of light from the cabin windows played out on to the frozen desert, raising monstrous shadows which raced away to the mountains. But above was a sight to take his breath away. A huge blue-green curtain rippled slowly across half the sky, fringed at its lower icebound edge by luminous flares of yellow and red, as though ignited by white-hot icebergs. The ripples spread across the sky as if the curtain were ruffled by a gentle breeze, or some unseen hand was painting the heavens gold.

Joshua lowered his hood to listen. He felt an almost instant pinch of frost on his ears. What he heard was a whistle, not a whisper, and it came, not from the heavens above, but from the deck, close by. He turned to see Simva's lips pouring out a melody that answered in gentleness the wafting overhead. She saw the question in his eyes, and broke off her tune to indicate, through gestures, that her whistling brought the evanescent tracery closer. He grinned. This must be Simva getting her own back for the pudding business: but when he turned back to face them he saw the lights *had* come closer. He reached out a hand, as if to caress them, then recognised on his outstretched palm familiar starshapes – Ursa Major, the Great Bear – that the captain had taught him in his navigation classes. His father always called it 'T' plough.'

Joshua found the two end stars in the plough's blade, and followed the line they made upwards, ignoring now the display of lights. He'd had Yorkshire snow and a Yorkshire dog at his feet the last time he did this, a year before. He found himself craning back further than ever he had at Whitby or any waypoint on his voyage north. Up and up and up went the line, to end at last in Polaris, the Pole Star. Joshua closed one eye and turned in a circle, one way and then the other, until he was sure.

This star, as constant a marker as his own instinct, had called and guided him northward since before his escape from Whitby. It had confirmed his own sense of where his father was and where he had to go. And now it was almost directly overhead. He was no nearer finding his father and he could go no further north. What more could he do? What better things could he hope for now? And what would happen when spring came, and the ice broke up, and his new-found home the *Aurora*, and new-found kin her crew, went south? What then for him? What then for his father?

'What then?' Joshua asked, first in a whisper, and then over and over in a rising shout to the stars, 'What then?' till Simva led him below to welcome warmth but an equal absence of answers.

Part 5
Greenland's Icy Mountains

Chapter 27

Winter wore on and on until it seemed eternal. Unrelieved darkness, hostile gales and bitter biting cold trapped the crew on board the *Aurora*, except for brief excursions when the wind dropped. Even then, when it wasn't shrieking its fury, the blizzard's ghostly moaning backed every aspect of their lives.

The captain used all his ingenuity to keep his crew as active as he could, both in body and mind. In all but the harshest weather he mustered them each day on deck, and had them dance under their improvised shelter, though he could only tempt them into it by offering grog at beginning and end. Donald Lewis and Bob

Barrow took turns to provide music on a penny whistle, while the crew hornpiped and reeled and jigged in the little ice-free space they had cleared.

One morning, just as they finished their jig and quickly quaffed their grog, the clouds that had hung about for weeks parted to reveal again the starlight, still unfamiliar in the middle of the day. But they revealed something more: a dim purple-orange glow in the southern sky, like a bruise on the edge of the heavens. Mr Colbeck raised his mug: 'Here comes the sun!' Everyone else raised their mugs too but any cheers they offered up were half-hearted.

Each day after that the whole crew scanned the southern sky at the same time, all of them impatient at how slowly the glow grew in brightness. Their dancing was more enthusiastic now, the penny whistle piped louder, and the work about the ship took on a new briskness.

A week later the unmistakable upper edge of the sun peeped over the horizon for the first time all year. The captain ordered double grog all around and this time there was nothing muted about the cheers that rang around the ship.

But the following noon, straining to see more, the crew fell into a puzzled silence when no sun came at all. ''Twas refraction, boys, no more. We must wait a little yet,' said the captain. Disappointment hung around them like a sea-fog in the doldrums.

Nathaniel Bridge rubbed his knees and winced. He had fallen during the hornpipe, as he did most mornings. ''Tis not the waitin' that troubles me, sir. ''Tis the dancin' we must do betimes.' He was only half-joking. 'I have no ear for a tune.'

The captain suppressed a grin. 'That you have no ear for a tune is plain from your attempts at singing, Mr Bridge. And it is when you combine grog and ice with your clumsy jigging that you find yourself asprawl, much to all our amusement.'

'Then am I promoted to ship's jester, sir?'

'No, Mr Bridge, you are not. I do not have you dance for the good of your ears or the merriment of your messmates. 'Tis for the strength of your legs, and arms, and back, for we shall soon have need of them to sail this vessel again, and I fear our strength has ebbed this long winter.'

'Aye sir, that it has. But I fear no hornpipe will bring it back.'

The captain was still smiling. He enjoyed banter, as did most of the crew, who were listening in while pretending not to. 'Would you put your strength to shipwork, Mr Bridge?'

'I would.' Bridge was smiling now too.

'Very well. While we wait for the sun we will work.' He turned to the rest of the crew. 'Mr Colbeck! Mr Hobbs! Prepare to raise our masts! It is high time we made this a ship once more.'

For the rest of that day, and the following morning, the crew chipped accumulated ice from the masts and spars stowed on deck, and then raised them, stage by stage, until they scraped the sky once more. Joshua joined in as vigorously as the rest, beating ice from the frozen-stiff ropes. The captain drew him aside, out of earshot.

'We shall be sailing south ere long, Compass Murphy, but I have no doubt we will be back. You are young but you have learned fast in a hard school, and I would have you join my crew, if you would. You could come aboard the regular way, by the gangplank, and have a share in our catch. What say you?'

Joshua twisted a rope into a neat coil while he considered. Eventually he spoke. 'I have no thought of my future, sir, other than finding my father.'

'I know. And none could have pursued the search as vigorously as you have. But ask yourself this: what if the *Lindisfarne* got free to sail south just as we became beset? What if he has waited a winter in Whitby for you? What if he is standing on the harbour wall as the *Aurora* comes in, and sees you waving from the bows?'

Joshua dropped the rope. He hadn't considered this at all. He straightened, to look the captain in the eye. 'Then we will work our farm, or crew some ship, as we choose, Captain. But we will do it together.'

'A good answer, lad. All I ask is that you consider my offer.' The captain turned away to the stern, as Joshua went back to his ropes, whipping them harder and harder against the deck. Questions crowded round in his mind, but the only answers were the thwacks that echoed back from the ice. What more can I do to find him? *Thwack*! What if I fail? *Thwack*! What will I do? *Thwack*! Where will I go? *Thwack*!

By the next day's dancing the masts were fully up. Joshua had forgotten how tall they were, and in the hornpipe fell over twice from always looking up. None of the crew laughed louder than Nathaniel Bridge, who was already pleased to know it would be the last dance of winter. Joshua shunned the grog that followed, and when the crew crowded round the grog tub, he scrambled, unobserved, up the ratlines to his familiar barrel.

This time it was no refraction, no mirage that greeted him. The sun rose slowly, casting huge spindly mast-shadows on the pinkened ice, yet giving no warmth from its watery light. When it had risen to its zenith, not half above the horizon, he yelled down, startling his shipmates below.

'The sun is back!' he yelled. 'The sun is back!' But he was answered by puzzled stares and questioning shouts. He climbed back down to persuade them he'd seen the dawn, but when he pointed to the horizon all he saw was the same glow as before.

He frowned, and raced back up the mast, then laughed out loud when he neared the top and realised he could see the sun from his height while it remained hidden from the deck. He scuttled up and down the rigging making the sun rise as he climbed and set as he descended, over and over and over, to make up for the long dark night now ended, and all the missed twilights of winter.

Chapter 28

The coming of the sun transformed the world, and gave an answer to one of Joshua's rope-thwack questions. He accepted there was nothing more he could do now to find his father, at least not until the *Aurora* got free: and meanwhile he must hunt, not for a missing ship, but for seal and walrus and fish.

With the new light and the beginnings of warmth, came the first glimpses of open water since autumn. Narrow leads opened and closed, but so far away from the ship they could only be seen from the mast-head. Joshua watched from his barrel for the dappling glint of sunlight on water, or the wreaths of frost-smoke which rose from the surface as distant tell-tales. 'Open lead!' he yelled, again and again. 'Ten miles, nor' nor' east . . . seven miles, west by south . . . nine miles, due north.' All his navigation skills, hard-earned in the captain's cabin, were needed now but he couldn't help wishing he had listened harder.

Hopeful hunting trips raced off to the nearest leads. Joshua had to rush down the rigging to be ready to join them. But however fast they set off, and however hard they marched, the stretches of open water were always so far from the ship that they were no longer open when reached. The pack ice always closed up again, and often so firmly that some began to doubt Joshua's claim there had ever been a lead there at all.

Frustration, as well as hunger, began to eat away at them. There was open water all around, but never near the ice encased ship. The seal and walrus it promised lay always tantalisingly out of reach, and the galley stores grew as thin as the crew's bellies.

One morning Joshua, who was on watch as always, winced as the hunger pangs hit. Rations had been reduced again. At first he didn't notice the glitter away to the west, but when he did all his pains vanished in an instant. 'Open lead!' he shouted. 'Right nearby! Four miles at most!' He was out of the barrel before he'd finished speaking, and down the rigging in a flash. He had laid his hunting harpoon against the base of the mast in readiness, and now slung it over his shoulder as he raced across the deck and down the ladder on to the ice, not bothering to wait for his crewmates. They can follow well enough, he thought. Those that believe me at least.

He half-walked, half-ran across the rippled ice in the direction of the lead. Nothing of it could be seen from the surface. A quick glance over his shoulder confirmed that a hunting party had set off in his footsteps, and he guessed they would catch him up just as he neared the lead. He pressed on, determined to get there first.

A thin wisp of frost-smoke acted as his beacon after a mile or so, but as he approached it thinned out further and vanished. Joshua took this to mean the lead had already closed, but even as his heart sank his legs pushed him on harder. After another mile he crested a small pressure ridge, and there was the lead below him, already dusted with a dense crop of ice flowers. Remnant patches of open water still smoked, and there, beside one of them, lay a solitary seal. It dozed lazily, no doubt enjoying a rare sunning, but Joshua knew it would be wary and watchful, if only for bears, and he had to be very careful not to alarm it.

He moved slowly and smoothly, freezing fast whenever the seal looked his way, and never taking his eyes off it as he approached and unslung his harpoon. He knew his crewmates might burst upon them any moment and scare his prize away, but he knew too, from his experience of the autumn, that he had to take his time to stand a chance. He was getting in range now, convinced that the seal must hear his pounding heart, as he raised his harpoon to strike. Another two steps, maybe three, he thought. I have to be sure.

The silence shattered. First came the whistle as a harpoon shot past him, then the sickening thud as it hit home, and the seal's awful cry of pain and surprise and fear, almost drowned by shouts of triumph behind. *Inuit* shouts.

He turned to see Simva and her father running up. Her father went straight past to the seal, his new knife at the ready, while Simva bounded up to hug him and rub noses. He didn't shrink away. She pointed at his harpoon and mimicked his stealthy approach. The seal might not have seen him but she and her father clearly had. She burst into giggles, only stopping when she saw the frown that said he took his hunting seriously. She hugged him again, just as the *Aurora* party crested the pressure ridge.

266

''Ey-up, Bob,' said Nathaniel Bridge. 'So that's why 'e ran off so quick. Yon lad's been chasin' Eskimo girls, not huntin' seal.'

Bob Barrow grinned at Joshua's renewed embarrassment. Everyone was laughing at him today. 'But judgin' by t' blood over there I reckon 'e's found both.'

There were greetings all round, amid which Joshua felt Bob Barrow's big hand on his shoulder, and a gruff whisper in his ear. 'Well done, lad. I'll follow you huntin' anywhere.' All Joshua's embarrassment vanished.

Simva's father handed them half the seal. Winter had been hard on Inuit and *kabloonah* alike, but he sensed the hunger in the men he'd met, and knew their need was as great as his. He invited them to visit his camp, but they declined, being too keen to get back to *Aurora* and cook up some dinner. Joshua, no less hungry than the rest, was disappointed, but promised Simva he would call as soon as he could.

Chapter 29

The next day Joshua was lead-spotting as usual, but only bothering to look in one direction – towards the Inuit camp. If leads opened up elsewhere he didn't want to know, however close by they were. The morning dragged on but just before noon he saw what he'd waited for. 'Open lead to the nor' east!' he yelled to those below. 'A big one . . . nine miles off, I'd say.'

A large hunting party – ten men, two sleds, and one eager boy – set off, in the direction Joshua had indicated. They walked fast, not saying much, each man absorbed in his thoughts. Joshua felt a tug on his harpoon. 'What's this?' asked Donald Lewis, at his shoulder. Neither broke stride, but Joshua swung the harpoon over his head and handed it over.

Donald Lewis examined it as he walked. Joshua had cut it down, attached a loop of twine as a sling, and polished and sharpened the blade till it looked like a butcher's knife – which, in a way, it was. But what Donald Lewis was admiring was the handiwork all along the shaft. Every inch of wood was covered by elaborate carvings in the Inuit style. There were bears and whales and walrus. There was an igloo and a whaling boat and, right next to the blade, a ship under full sail. 'You've been busy, young Murphy,' he said, obviously impressed.

Joshua tried not too smile too widely. 'It was a long winter,' he replied.

'Aye, so it was.' They fell silent for a time. 'But this is a short summer, and unless these leads open nearer to the ship I fear we are doomed to remain here longer yet.'

He said nothing more, but Joshua's thoughts raced ahead. It had never occurred to him until then that they might not break free, and he did not know what he felt about it. To stop himself thinking too much he began looking about. The men guessed he was searching for seals; only he knew that though the figures – the figure – he sought might be dressed in seal skin, they – she

– walked upright, and had liquid laughter, and the silkiest black hair he had ever seen.

But all he saw was barren ice in every direction, glistening in the afternoon sun. Bob Barrow, at the head of the group, turned to signal a halt, with an emphatic finger to his lips. It was an utterly windless day, and any sound would carry for miles to alert their prey. Joshua crouched to the ice like the men around him, thinking that at least the lack of wind meant the seals wouldn't smell them. He hadn't had a bath for six months.

They had reached the lead. Some of the men looked at Joshua. He didn't know if this was to acknowledge that he'd been right again, or out of surprise he hadn't seen it first. He stopped thinking about warm baths and stared across. This lead *was* big, large enough to contain free-floating islands of ice. One or two had likely-looking seal-shapes lolling atop them.

After a whispered conference the party divided in two, to head in opposite directions along the edge of the lead, and with an arrangement to meet at that same point in four hours, or, failing that, back at the ship. Joshua made sure he was in the group heading east towards the Inuit camp.

They were in luck, and within an hour had

bagged two big seals, which was as much as their sledge could carry. The men smiled and chatted freely as they loaded their catch: there was no need for quiet now. 'What now?' asked Nathaniel Bridge of Mr Colbeck, who led the group. 'Sit on our behinds gettin' froz while we wait for t' others, or 'ead on back to t' ship?'

Mr Colbeck paused. He looked around the horizon, giving himself time to think, but just as he opened his mouth Joshua, not liking either option, piped up. 'We could visit the Inuit camp, could we not, sir?'

Mr Colbeck closed his mouth again and stared at him.

Joshua persisted. 'We owe them season's greetings . . . and half a seal.'

'Lad's right,' said Bob Barrow. 'And it's not far off.'

Joshua was in like a knife. 'A mile and a half. Over there.' He pointed to the east.

Colbeck smiled at last. 'All right then. A visit it is.'

Joshua crossed his fingers inside his mittens, hoping that Simva was in. For the first time that day he was in front, striding out across the ice. They soon saw the little gaggle of tents and igloos, just off the sea ice. The camp looked impossibly fragile from this distance, but it was clear from its bustle that the Inuit had survived the winter well.

The barking of dogs greeted the visitors as they drew up. A posse of tiny children, made almost spherical by their thick furs, trotted towards them, babbling what must have been nonsense in any tongue. Four or five adults stepped out of their tents, or broke off their work on the sledges, and welcomed the men of the *Aurora* with broad grins and admiring glances at the seals they dragged.

Joshua's eyes darted from one Inuit face to the next, with a deepening sense of disappointment. A figure from the back of the group strode forward and lowered his hood to reveal himself as Simva's father. Joshua brightened; he had never seen Simva and her father apart, so she must be somewhere nearby. He tried not to look around too obviously.

Bob Barrow muttered something to Mr Colbeck, turned to his sledge, and dragged the smaller of the two seals it bore towards the gathering. He laid it at the feet of Simva's father, with a flourish that indicated a debt had been repaid, and generosity rewarded.

Donald Lewis looked aghast. 'I caught yon beast,' he said, in pained tones. 'You cannot go givin' it away as if it were a mackerel or sprat.'

Mr Colbeck drew him aside, but not so far off that Joshua couldn't overhear. 'Fear not, Donald. Your catch will soon be nestling in your belly, and all the cooking done for you. We owe them half a seal: we give them a whole one: they cook it and feed it back to us. Everybody's happy.'

A half-smile spread slowly across Donald Lewis's face, but Mr Colbeck was not done. He was suddenly serious. 'But think on, Donald. Nigh on half the whales we caught, whose oil is stowed on our ship, were harpooned by Bob here, or by me. That don't make 'em his, or mine. They are *ours*.' He waved his arm to indicate his crewmates. 'We all have a share, even you.'

Joshua applauded the sentiment, even though he was keenly aware that as a stowaway he was the only one on board the *Aurora* who did not have a share in her catch. He hung back while his shipmates gathered round the cooking tent and bantered with the Inuit. He was not hungry; at least not for food. He strolled to the edge of the camp, wary of the dogs tethered there. He couldn't be sure how long their leashes were, and he guessed some saw him as a stranger, despite his anorak and the sledging trips he had taken them on in the autumn.

'Psssst!' something hissed behind him. He thought for an instant it was a dog trying to scare him, but when he looked round he saw Simva, beckoning from behind a rocky outcrop.

He greeted her with a grin, trying to look casual, but she grasped his arm and pulled him behind the rock. 'Hey!' he cried, till she quieted him. That, and the way she peered round the rock toward the camp soon told him she had plans she had to keep secret from her father and the rest. He nodded his understanding and followed her as she led him away.

There was open water here, almost up to the shoreline, and when they rounded a little headland Joshua saw five or six dark shapes drawn up on the ice-edge. They were far too thin for seals, but there could be no doubt their natural home was the water. Joshua ran his hands over the nearest boat, marvelling at its delicacy and elegance. It was made from hide, oiled to translucency and stretched drum-tight over a framework made of bone. The outer shell thrilled to his touch and the whole vessel rocked at the slightest pressure. It was impossibly light, and nothing at all like the heavy wooden skiffs Joshua knew from Whitby harbour. Hull and deck were one continuous surface, totally enclosed but for a tiny central cockpit. Hunting implements – a harpoon, a knife, a coil of twine, an air bladder – were lashed fore and aft. A double-ended paddle made of bone lay on the ice nearby, with hide mittens attached.

'Kayak!' said Simva.

'Kay-ak,' Joshua repeated, absent-mindedly, as he examined the vessel. He wondered why Simva hadn't shown him before, and why it was a secret now. 'Kay-ak.'

Simva picked up the paddle and thrust it into his grasp. 'We . . . go!' she said. Her words may have been hesitant, but there was no doubt about her meaning. Joshua took the paddle at once. 'We go!' he grinned back. It would be so good to be afloat again.

He watched her launch her own kayak, bring it alongside the ice-edge, and slip into the seat space, sliding her legs up into the bows, and using her paddles to balance. Only when she got out again did Joshua realise she'd been demonstrating the techniques involved. He kicked himself for not watching closely enough. Together they launched the kayak she had chosen for him. When they picked it up it seemed so light it could float in air, never mind on water, and when they lowered it to the surface it quivered like a live thing released from a cage.

Simva showed him how to stabilise it by laying the paddle across the deck while he slid himself in. Even with his white-knuckle grip and her helping hands the fragile craft lurched violently as he fumbled his feet into the bows. He held on to the ice-edge for security while Simva returned to her own kayak, into which she slipped like a water vole entering its burrow. 'Watch!' she cried, as she took up her paddle. She held it up with both hands and motioned him to follow. Reluctantly he let go the ice-edge and did as she bade him. The kayak reflected back to him all the tension and tremor in his worried muscles: but it didn't turn over as he feared.

Simva twisted slowly from side to side, pushing ahead each shoulder in turn, with the paddle still held above the water. Joshua copied her and began to relax as he felt the boat beneath him move. She took him through a range of exercises before she lowered her paddle to the water. At first she just touched it, laying the blade upon the slate-grey surface like a duck washing its wings, first one side and then the other. Joshua copied her carefully, growing so fast in confidence that he anticipated her dipping the paddle in and pulling. He was amazed at the effect. The kayak responded like a pigeon released from its loft, or a whippet from its trap, taking off with an eagerness for movement he found scary and exhilarating at one and the same time.

After three or four tentative strokes there was no stopping him. His kayak flashed past Simva's in a blur of whirling arms, splashing paddles and bubbling laughter. Simva paddled after him, fearing the worst, and with reason, for she hadn't yet shown him how to stop. It was only when a gently spinning ice floe loomed dead ahead that Joshua realised this too. He stabbed his port paddle deep into the water and held it there as a brake. Immediately the kayak slewed round violently and heeled hard over. Freezing water poured in and sprayed around his face as he spluttered his surprise. He was surely going under.

He thrashed at the paddle, but all it seemed to do was dig deeper still. There was a sudden lurch, and then his craft began to right itself, but only sluggishly, being now half-filled with water. When he was sure he was not going to sink he let out his breath in a great cloud, and shook the water from his sodden hair, trying to work out what he had done to get upright again. It was only when he saw the bow of Simva's kayak next to his that he realised he had not done it himself at all. He turned, and saw worry and anger and amusement flit in turn across her face, like clouds across the sun on a blustery Yorkshire day.

She said nothing. They both knew he had

learnt his lesson. Simva held out one hand, palm down, and signalled with a downward movement that he had to go more slowly. He nodded solemnly, and after that his lessons began in earnest.

Chapter 30

Joshua took every chance he could get to visit the camp, and Simva showed him in turn all the manoeuvres of the kayak: getting in, getting out, coming alongside the ice, paddling straight, steering and stopping, and then, when at last he was ready, a complete underwater roll.

When he had mastered all of this they set off through the widening maze of leads for his first kayak hunting trip. Joshua knew this was a privilege rarely accorded a *kabloonah* man, never mind a mere boy. He kept it as secret from his crew as Simva did from her family, and this intensified his delight.

He licked his lips as he paddled after Simva.

He was dry mouthed with anticipation, but the taste of salt splashed on his face took him back to his early days at the *Aurora*'s bowsprit, heading north to Orkney. It seemed like a lifetime ago.

They cruised along the ice-edge in tandem, till Simva signalled a stop. Water dripped from their paddles into the oily calm, then slowed till the only sounds were their own breathing, and the distant rumble of calving glaciers. The two kayaks slid over the pewter sea like companion raindrops down a window pane. Simva looked at him with a smile as deep as a glacier crevasse.

They scanned the ice for any sign of seal, but none were about today. They paddled and drifted another mile or two, till Joshua's eyes began to hurt from his staring. He turned to face away from the sun, and Simva, hearing his sharp intake of breath, turned too. Together they saw, on the far side of the now-narrowed lead, a solitary dark silhouette, drawn up, unsuspecting, on the ice. It just *had* to be a seal.

Joshua set off at once till stopped by Simva's urgent hiss. She mimed her plan: they would paddle back the way they had come, then straight across the lead, and drift downwards with the tide to close upon their dozing quarry. Joshua nodded. Again he had been too impatient, too direct, and again he was humbled to have her point it out. But he knew she was right, and he paddled along behind her as smoothly as he could.

Simva stopped paddling when the creature was still two hundred yards away: or one cable off, as Joshua had been taught to measure distance. She balanced her paddle on the deck before her and began to unlash her harpoon and its coiled-up line. Joshua did likewise as the two kayaks drifted along the fringe of ice. Slowly he raised the harpoon to hold it by his shoulder, his elbow resting on deck. He never took his eyes off the sleeping beast. From fifty yards away he could make out four or five angry red scars running down its side, in parallel lines an inch or two apart, crimson witness to a close encounter with a killer whale. 'You're a lucky seal,' Joshua whispered under his breath. He tightened his grip on his harpoon. 'Are you lucky still?'

The animal turned, sensing something, and only then did Joshua see it wasn't a seal at all. A single white tusk projected forwards from the left side of its upper jaw, for six feet or more, with a spiral groove carved on to its ivory surface. A narwhal! thought Joshua. He'd heard tales of these legendary creatures, but the sailors who told them went on so much about sea-unicorns and mermaids he hadn't believed them.

Simva caught his eye. She had seen plenty narwhals and never caught one, but she laid her harpoon along her deck and nodded her wish that he should strike first. Joshua's gaze flicked back to the now-wary animal. His fingers curled round the shaft of his harpoon, while with his other hand he checked the line was smoothly flaked out, so it wouldn't snag when he struck. He looked down at the water, to see how the wind moved him over it; then across at the ice-edge, to check the set of the tide; and then back at the narwhal. *His* narwhal. Slowly he raised his harpoon hand, then drew it back past his shoulder, then paused. A little closer yet . . . he thought. Another few feet.

The narwhal turned to stare at him. Sunlight flashed off its astonishing tusk, and red glistened thickly in the slashes on its side. Only then did Joshua notice the blood trickling down to gather in a pool under the creature's body: these slashes were fresh. The narwhal made no move to escape, and Joshua made none to strike. He gazed at the tusk, and the blood, and the wounds, red-letter evidence of its struggle to survive, and he knew he would not – could not – kill the creature. He turned to Simva and laid down his harpoon arm, hoping she understood.

She didn't. She frowned at him and raised her

own harpoon, but before she struck the silence suddenly erupted in an explosion of surge and spray, and a cloud of oily breath, as a huge black and white shape burst through the surface behind them and crashed back down with a massive splash. Joshua glimpsed fins spread wide, twenty feet from tip to tip, but what chilled him most was the sight of a huge gaping mouth, home to scores of hungry teeth, below a tiny eye which glinted darkly amid the surf.

'*Orca*!' yelled Simva, as she took up her paddles and made for the ice, urging Joshua to follow. As he splashed furiously behind her, out-pacing the waves raised by the orca's breach, Joshua tried not to think how much they must resemble a pair of seals to a hungry whale. They bumped up against the ice and scrambled out of their kayaks faster than ever before, then hauled them up and dragged them away from the edge. A dim dream-memory of black and white monsters butting up through ice, hungry for his dog, haunted Joshua, who only felt safe when he was sure the ice was too thick for even the biggest whale to break.

Almost unnoticed in the commotion, the narwhal shuffled off to the ice-edge, an oily crimson trail marking its path. It seemed more prepared to take its chances with the whale in the water than these amphibious hunters on the ice. Joshua watched as it slipped into the steely steaming water with barely a ripple. He scanned the surface all around for the tell-tale high fin of the orca, but all he saw was a trail of bubbles as the narwhal dived and sped away. 'You might not be a seal,' said Joshua, out loud this time, 'but you are lucky.'

Chapter 31

The rat-a-tat rattle and rasping buzz of carpentry filled the ship and roused Joshua from his fo'c'sle berth. For days now, whenever he returned from his kayak trips, he had been dimly aware that old Benjamin Watt was busy below deck at his bench: but he had dismissed it as mere barrel business. Now it was obvious something much bigger was going on.

Heavy timbers lay about the deck, which was sprinkled with sawdust and strewn about with shavings. Benjamin Watt and some of the crew were sawing them to size and hammering them together into a sturdy framework like a heavy farm gate. Joshua tried to work out what it was, but only when he saw the runners did he guess.

Bob Barrow stopped hammering and looked up. Sweat stained his shirt and dripped from his brow, to darken the wood he had newly bared. 'All right, lad?' he asked, reaching across for more nails from Nathaniel Bridge.

'That's the biggest sledge I've ever seen,' said Joshua.

'Big enough. A bigger un yet is takin' shape on t' quarterdeck.'

'But why?'

Nathaniel Bridge broke in. ''Tis the north pole, ain't it?' There was a new hardness in his voice. 'Who else would ye build a sledge for but Father Christmas? We are his elves, workin' all hours for a ha'porth o' grog.'

'Cannot you tell, Joshua?' Bob Barrow asked. What had been an open secret amongst the crew seemed to have passed the boy by completely. He laid down his hammer and stood up, arching backwards with a wince to ease his aching back. He raised one arm and swept it past the horizon. 'Ice,' he said. 'Nothin' but ice, son, when 'tis past midsummer and there should be water all about us.'

Joshua knew only too well how far the *Aurora* was from open water. He paddled mile after mile in the kayak, but the leads never took him anywhere near the ship. Long homeward trudges, dragging his catch on a hunting sledge, showed how firmly encased she was; but he always thought it was just a matter of time before she was free.

Bob Barrow shook his head. 'Season marches on; unless we're released soon, we'll not be released at all. And though you've hunted like you were born to it, we are not victualled for another winter frozen in.' He patted his handiwork. 'This is our way out.'

'And leave t' ship behind?' It seemed such a betrayal.

'If need be. Fear not: we'll not leave her until we absolutely must. But if – or when – that time comes, 'tis ready we must be. And that's why we're workin', me and Grumpy here, and t' other elves.'

'What are these?' Joshua pointed to two huge saws laid on deck, each of them at least eight feet long, with enormous thick blades and teeth as vicious as those of any killer whale. If they were made to cut wood it was wood from no tree he had ever seen, and this was an utterly tree-less land, green only in name.

'Ice saws. If a lead opens near enough we can cut our way toward it. But t' nearest lead is so far off these would be blunted long before we got there, even if our strength weren't.'

New uncertainties piled up on top of old in Joshua's mind, like fresh snow settling on an ice-field. He fell silent and his gaze turned away to the north, and Simva's camp, as his thoughts folded inward. If the ice opened and the ship got free, she'd soon be sailing south to Whitby. If the ice held fast she would be abandoned to her fate while her crew sledged to safety. Either way he would be leaving: and he did not want to go. He felt more at home in this icy kingdom than anywhere else on earth. A candle of hope that he might yet find his father still flickered stubbornly within him; but he sensed something more, something inside telling him he *belonged* here, however cold and dark and dangerous it might get.

Chapter 32

The first thing Joshua heard when he woke was the silence. It was noisy enough within the tent, what with the walrus snores of Simva's father, and her grandfather's wheezy rasp: but outside all was still and silent and calm. He threw back the thick caribou fur cover that had kept him so warm and listened deeply, drinking it in.

For three days now the first blizzard of autumn had howled across the ice, shrieking down from the cliffs and threatening to tear away the tent where he, Simva, and her family took refuge. The cacophony of the storm reflected Joshua's inner turmoil. His whirling snowflake thoughts swirled in sharp contrast to the passive patience of Simva's family as they waited out the storm, just as they had so many before it. They put Joshua's restlessness down to him being a *kabloonah*, ill-suited to blizzard-bound waiting: but he knew otherwise. For this was his last visit, though he could not bring himself to say so.

Mr Hobbs had made it very clear when Joshua set off from *Aurora* for the camp, ostensibly to say his farewells. 'We'll take to the sledges in two days, son. Three at most. You must be back by then for we cannot wait. Do you understand?' There was no hint of the coming storm in the sky.

Joshua understood only too well, but was no nearer knowing what he would do. Now, with the storm blown out, the men of the *Aurora* would surely be setting off at once. If he was to go with them he had to go now.

He stepped out of the tent into crystal air and blinding light. Snow piled up against the windward sides of the tents and igloos, as bleary Inuit emerged from their narrow entrances like a company of moles. Sunlight bounced off the nearby cliffs and gilded the ice floes with silver and copper and gold. The snow-covered peak of a mountain across the fjord burned with reflected sunlight like a huge candle. Two gyrfalcons wheeled above it, in opposing spirals.

At his feet a bump in the snow wriggled and

writhed, then swelled and burst open to reveal a yawning dog. Other lumps nearby came to life, one by one, as the rest of the team emerged. They shook the snow from their fur and stood, enveloped in clouds of warm dog-breath, as they barked greetings at each other. They barked at Joshua too, but this was a welcome not a warning, as if he now belonged. He thought about Nelson, who used to bark at him in much the same way. Suddenly Joshua knew he could not just walk away and trudge back to his ship. At the very least he had to imprint this place in his mind and mark his presence in it before he left.

He looked around for Simva. She was surprised to see his eyes aglisten, and the sadness in his face, as he took her arm. In a halting mixture of Inuit and English and gesture he conveyed to her the fact he had to go. She'd expected it more than he had, but even so it was her eyes' turn to moisten now.

Joshua looked past her shoulder to the candle mountain, still flaring brightly. He raised a hand to point at it. 'We . . . go!' he declared. Simva nodded to show she understood why, and smiled at him. 'We . . . go!'

After breakfast they harnessed a dog team and set off as if to go hunting, but once away from the camp they turned north to the mountain. The dogs were unfamiliar with this route, and hesitated in their eager pulling, but only for a moment, and after an hour or two they had drawn the sledge across the frozen fjord to the narrow ice-beach where the mountain reached the water.

Simva re-rigged the dog harnesses to tie the animals in a line, each with its own space. The dogs watched closely as Joshua and Simva set off on foot, then one by one they turned one or two circuits to trample the snow, and nonchalantly curled up, thickly furred tails laid across their muzzles.

To Joshua's surprise Simva was a less sure-footed climber than he was. At their first rest she explained that climbing was not something the Inuit did, there being no need, and no food to be had by it. Joshua unslung his harpoon and showed her how to use it as a staff, and when he was sure she had the knack, he turned to lead the way, stopping every so often to pick out the route.

To his relief the climb was straightforward, and the weather held. He led Simva over gently sloping snow-fields, skirting tumbled ice-falls and working past rocky precipices. They rose steadily higher as the map of the fjord fingers and knuckled mountains unfolded behind them. Joshua did not want to look back until he was at the top, and directed all his attention ahead. What was it his father used to say as they scrambled over the Whitby cliffs? *Onward and upward.* Exactly.

He stopped to teach Simva these new English words, which she giggled back to him for the rest of the climb. 'On-wad!' she said whenever the going was flat, and 'Up-wad!' at every vertical scramble. Many on-wads and up-wads later they found themselves resting once more, not far below the summit. Joshua examined it carefully to find a route for this, the last leg. Still he would not look round. He was saving that.

It was easier than he thought, and in another half-hour they stood, side by side, on the summit, which now revealed itself as no more than a foothill to a huge mountain range stretching away to the horizon. Simva, who had never seen anything from a height like this, gasped as she stared about. She knew the land and water below so well, but only in two dimensions. She sang out when she saw her family's camp, betrayed by a light curl of blubber smoke twisting up from a cooking vent.

Joshua was overheating from the exertion of the climb. He took off his anorak, wondering if anyone had ever stood where they stood now, and wished he had a flag. He peered at the holes in the old guernsey smock he wore underneath. It was falling to bits. He pulled his right arm out of the sleeve. 'Simva!' he called, and flapped the empty sleeve at her when she turned.

'Hold it,' he said. 'Tight.' She gripped the sleeve in both hands, even though she had no idea what he was up to. 'Now pull!' As soon as she did so he pulled backwards himself. Both of them were laughing out loud at the absurdity of it – a tug of war at the top of a mountain at the top of the world, and all for a guernsey still worn by one of the tuggers.

Suddenly the salt-weakened stitching parted and the sleeve ripped away. Both of them fell backwards in the snow, Joshua's pale and skinny arm waving above his head like a filleted fish. There was a dull distant thud as a snow-field broke free in an avalanche. It thundered down the sunward slopes of the neighbouring mountain. Their laughter, which may have triggered it, died in their throats and they watched, in silence now, as a boiling cloud roared into the valley below.

Suddenly sobered, Joshua shivered and put his anorak back on. He lashed the sleeve to the shaft of his harpoon which would serve as a flagstaff, now his hunting days were done. He planted this firmly in the ice at the very summit. Simva helped him pile more snow round the base and stamp it down hard. When they were done Joshua stood up straight and saluted. Simva copied him.

His sleeve hung limply in the windless air, though he knew it would unravel instantly in the next blizzard that came. Joshua did not care, for it meant that the fibres of his guernsey, stained with his sweat, flecked with his blood, and imbued with his tears, would be blown from here across all the ice and mountains and sea of this country he had come to love. Whatever happened next, some of him would stay here for ever.

A breath of wind puffed the sleeve-flag straight and revealed behind it a jagged zig-zag lead, thrusting away from the shore into the sea-ice, as if a monstrous thunderbolt had been hurled down from the mountain-top. The blizzard must have cracked the ice, and now, as the tide worked on it, chunks broke off and were swept away. Even as they watched the lead widened and lengthened, driving towards the south. Towards the *Aurora*.

He could make out the familiar masts and hull of his ship in the distance. Beyond it, crawling slowly south away from the vessel, were two strange bumbling beetle-creatures attended by insect-men.

Joshua was shivered to his soul, and let out a great wail of anguish. 'The sledges!' he cried. 'They've abandoned her!' He couldn't bear to think that they had abandoned him too. 'They're leaving her and they can't see she could still get free.' He turned to Simva, who struggled to understand the emotions contorting his face. When, more calmly, he pointed to the dog-team far below, and said simply, 'Down. Fast,' she understood perfectly and followed his already half-running feet as fast as she could go.

Chapter 33

They hurtled downwards like a pair of snow-balls, slipping and slithering and tumbling in turns, trying desperately not to think about avalanches. What had taken them careful hours going up took reckless minutes down. Soon they found themselves on a large, gently shelving snow-field, not far above the sea ice. It was Simva who noticed they were not alone. When Joshua turned to follow her terrified stare all he saw at first was whiteness, but part of it was large and mobile and lumbering towards them with astonishing speed and a fearsome roar.

'*Nanook*!' yelled Simva. If their descent had thus far been reckless, now it became a panic-stricken headlong plunge. But it was no good: the bear was gaining rapidly. Joshua could hear its breathing and the heavy falls of its feet on the crusted snow. He did not dare look round, and all he saw in front was the sharp line where the snow-field stopped abruptly at a cliff edge. He did not know how it would end – a bone-crushing fall, or the pounce of the bear – but either way his time was up. He closed his eyes and kept running.

The bear's roar and the smell of its breath filled the air all around him. Just as it swung at him with a huge forepaw, Simva grabbed his right arm and yanked him sideways. A violent thump in his back flung him over the edge, and he found himself in space. So it would be the fall, and not the bear, which won him. At least he wasn't alone.

He seemed to be in the air forever. And then, abruptly, he was embedded in something which was neither air nor jagged rocks and unforgiving ice. Whatever it was he could not breathe in it. He coughed and spluttered and thrashed about, them remembered to open his eyes. And saw the sun.

Far above, on the edge of the cliff, the bear roared down its impotent fury. Beside him lay Simva, still clutching his arm. Beneath lay thickly drifting snow, where the blizzard had piled it fifteen feet deep against the cliff face. Joshua sat up. It was only when he saw the spreading red stain in the patch where he had lain, and suddenly felt the sharp pain in his back, that he was sure he was really still alive.

Simva sat up too, and shouted something in Inuit at the bear. The only word Joshua made out was '*Nanook*!' and he guessed that the rest was Inuit swearing, not meant for *kabloonah* ears. The bear disappeared, but Joshua worried about it finding its way down, stung by her taunts into wreaking revenge on a half-caught boy and his mocking companion.

Simva examined his back, and showed him the three great tears the bear's claws had ripped in his anorak. His wounds were long, but not deep, and the cold soon stopped the bleeding and dulled the pain. They swopped anoraks, to keep his back well-covered, then looked about. They had lost their bearings in their headlong scramble and sudden fall, and even Simva was not sure which way to head to find the dogs. Eventually they settled on the left, and began picking their way along the foreshore.

Simva waved a hand to indicate the territory nearby. '*Nanook, nanook, nanook,*' she said, as if Joshua didn't know by now this was bear country. She stopped and made him watch her gestures as she repeated herself. For the first two '*nanooks*' she held her hand high above her head and growled the word. For the third she lowered her hand to knee-height and raised her voice to a squeak.

Now Joshua understood. This wasn't just bear country – it was where they bred. That was why the bear had been so fierce, why the Inuit didn't come, why the dogs thought it odd, and why Simva wasn't sure of her bearings. He looked at her steadily. She had known all this and still come with him. He was touched and wanted to show his appreciation. He held out his hand in a gesture she had come to know. They shook hands warmly as he tried to thank her for saving his life – again. He imagined that somehow she knew of the snow-blanket below when she'd pulled him away from the bear and over the cliff. She didn't understand his words, but guessed his meaning, and shook her head to tell him he'd got it wrong.

As they resumed walking, she went through an elaborate mime-show of Inuit life: hurling harpoons, hacking blubber, sawing snowblocks, and more. After every action she held up one hand – always the right – until he picked up her message: that she was right-handed. He frowned a so-what frown, till she grinned, put on her *nanook* scowl, and swiped at him. He jumped back and she swiped again, and again, and each time, he noticed, with her left hand.

He laughed. She was trying to tell him that bears were left-handed, and that was why she had pulled him aside when she did. He shook his head in smiling disbelief. She shrugged, knowing she was right, and waited till he least expected it before swiping again, this time with her other hand. She caught him on the shoulder and sent him sprawling.

After he got to his feet and dusted the snow from his anorak for the third time that day, he and Simva fell suddenly silent. As the exhilaration of their narrow escape faded, the urgency of their mission pressed in on them. They set off once more; faster this time.

Chapter 34

As they walked on through ever more unfamiliar territory both grew uneasy that they had chosen the wrong route. Joshua didn't like to say anything until he was sure, deferring to Simva's superior navigation skills, in her own land. He was just about to call a halt when he saw ahead something he knew did not belong.

On any beach near Whitby driftwood abounded and meant precious little. Here, in this woodless world, it bore a deadly significance. A shattered plank of painted wood lay upon the shore, well above the high water mark. Joshua ran up to it, and turned it over and over in search of any indicator of its origin, pleading for it to give up its secrets. He found none, and looked about for more. Simva spotted the next, equally mute piece, and further on they found more, all anonymous.

A low headland lay ahead. Joshua steeled himself for what might lie behind it and pressed on, while Simva held back. He had to find out.

It was as he feared. The next beach was strewn with the unmistakable wreckage of a substantial ship. Joshua ran from one splintered timber to another in a desperate search for any kind of clue, until he saw the upturned lifeboat right at the base of the cliff. He ran towards it and fell upon the stern, scraping away the ice that obscured her name until there could be no mistake. *Lindisfarne*. He had found his father's ship, though Lord knew not the way he wanted to.

Simva knew not to intrude, and watched as he fell to his knees and beat upon the lifeboat crying one word – *No!* – over and over. As he slumped, exhausted, and his weeping quieted, she heard something else behind it, and though she could not identify the sound, she knew there were bears close by.

She could hold back no more and approached to lay a hand upon his still-heaving shoulder. 'Yoshy,' she said as gently as she could. 'Yoshy . . .'

He looked up, and made no effort to hide the tears that streamed down his face.

'*Nanook*,' she said, as she indicated the bounds of the beach. '*Nanook*.'

Joshua nodded glumly, not really caring if the bears got him now. But he didn't want them to get her. He felt in his pocket before he remembered they had swopped anoraks. She saw this and pulled out from the pocket of his tattered anorak a knife, his scrimshaw, and some matches. She knew he carried his most precious possessions about his neck, but here and now these matches were most precious of all, at least to her.

They thawed some splinters of wood with body heat and breath until they had a little pile of kindling, and piled up other wood nearby. When there was enough Simva looked at Joshua who nodded sadly back. She tried the first match. It broke and fizzed off into the snow. There were two left in the box as she handed it back to him. He struck the next, and as it flared into life they crowded around and fed it shipwreck kindling.

With care and concentration they soon had a flickering fire, around which they piled more and more wood, to act as a windbreak and to thaw it out. The *Lindisfarne*'s timbers might not have saved her crew, but no bears would approach while there was wood to burn, and here they had plenty.

When he was sure the fire was well set, Joshua looked around. The sun had long disappeared behind the cliff, to leave the beach in shadow, and now the violet colour of the arctic autumn night crept across the sky. They weren't going anywhere till dawn. How far away would the sledges be by then? Would *nanook* find the dogs? He found it hard to care.

But they had to make some kind of shelter. With much effort they raised the upturned lifeboat, swung it round against the wind, and propped it up with stones and blocks of ice, so that its upper side faced the cliff. They moved the fire, brand by brand, nearer to the boat, and piled more wood ready, so they would not have to scavenge round a darkened bear-bound beach. They finally settled in the shelter of the boat to take what warmth they could from the fire and each other.

As the night wore on they had to pile more and more wood on the fire to keep frostbite at bay. The blaze intensified, growing brighter and brighter against the hardening dark, and revealed at its height something black in the bows of the boat.

Joshua retrieved it to examine by the light,

and he saw it was a book, with a cracked leather cover and frozen-together pages. Lettering had been embossed on the cover, most of it now lost, but he traced the indentations with his finger like a blind man, until he knew that he held in his hands the *Lindisfarne*'s log. Too nervous to trust it to frozen fingers near crackling flames, for an hour or more he warmed it under his anorak, until the pages began to separate. At around midnight he settled down to read, while Simva held a burning brand behind him to illuminate the pages.

Part 6
Breakout

Chapter 35

Joshua carefully turned the crackling pages until he came to a date engraved on his heart as deeply as the headstone lettering in Whitby graveyard. He began to read:

> 0900. Departed Whitby on ebb tide, making five knots in fresh SW breeze under fine skies. New sails sound, but leak in region of replaced timbers aft requires continuous pumping.

As he read on, the *Lindisfarne*'s journey merged with episodes of his own northward voyage on the *Aurora*, a year later. He wondered if the sea remembered the ships that passed and repassed across her surface, as skin recalled movement in wrinkles.

Becalmed in light fog, eight cables off St Abb's head. It had been clear when the *Aurora* sailed by, the headland revealed in all its forbidding grandeur. *Bass Rock passed at noon, Isle of May visible off port bow.* Joshua recalled the yellow-beaked gannets all around, plunging into the sea with folded wings, like golden-tipped white arrows raining from the sky.

But there was an ominous difference in the *Lindisfarne*'s passage, which recurred again and again in the log: she was leaking, and it was getting worse. *New leak forward at mainmast foot on starboard side. Two men pumping at all times. Repair work required Orkney.* The harbour pilot in the Ferry Inn back at Stromness had spoken to Joshua of the *Lindisfarne*'s leak. Joshua knew he had been right to be worried then, and promised to trust his instincts in future.

Beached by Stromness for repairs and re-caulking. New timbers sound but evidence of shipworm in nearby planking. Shipworm! A puff of breath flared grey-white in the freezing air, lit up by Simva's burning brand, as Joshua voiced the word. Just as all manner of vermin might eat away at the mighty beams of a church, and bring the roof crashing down, so were there marine borers, gribble and teredo, ever-ready to devour even the stoutest Yorkshire oak of any vessel that ventured unprotected into tropical waters. Joshua recalled his father's verdict at the condition in which the *Lindisfarne* had been returned to Whitby after a three-year exploration voyage in the Pacific. 'Not even copper-bottomed,' he had said, shaking his head. Only now did Joshua understand his anger.

But the repairs had worked. *Departed Stromness in light SW airs. Minimal leaking.* The terse entries that spanned the days and weeks to follow were little more than a list of abbreviations and numbers denoting wind speed, course and position, all now familiar from Joshua's winter lessons. It was so strange to be reading the words of a different captain, on a different vessel, whose wreckage now lay strewn all about.

Joshua turned the pages until he saw the first whale silhouette and thrilled to read, underneath it *Caught by Thomas Murphy, specksioneer*. There were many more whale-heads in the pages that followed, and although his father's name was not the only one to be honoured, it did appear most frequently. Joshua felt a glow of pride to know that, however much his father's trade repelled him, he excelled at it.

By any measure the *Lindisfarne*'s voyage was

a successful one, with almost twice as many barrels filled as the *Aurora*. As the season drew to its close, all aboard would have been thinking of their share. His father's dream – a farm of his own, a home for Joshua and himself – was close to fruition.

Then everything changed. The even-handed copperplate of the log thus far was suddenly replaced by a hasty scrawl, scratching out a terrible story which brought to life all Joshua's fears.

> *July 18th, 1030. Brace of sperm whale espied and boats launched. Thomas Murphy led his boat and two others far off to W in pursuit of large star-browed bull. William Budgett caught and killed smaller female.*
>
> *1230. Carcase lashed alongside and flensing preparations begun. No sign of Murphy's boats, but large male with star-shaped brow-patch broached close to ship. Budgett's boat made to relaunch, but whale drove directly toward ship at great speed, and all hands required to wear ship to port.*
>
> *1300. Damaging blows struck by whale on starboard side at fore and aft carcase-securing chains. Timbers started below. Taking water fast. Half remaining hands assigned to pumps*

and emergency repairs. Whale attacks continue, with further damage, until return of Thomas Murphy's boat. At great peril of his life Murphy draws up to carcase, climbs on to it and cuts it free from securing chains, then he and crew row it off from ship, pursued by fearsome threats from bull whale, and set it adrift astern. Whale breaks off attacks on ship and accompanies carcase with much displaying of flukes.

1430. All hands return to vessel to attend to damage. Serious leaks in region of ship-wormed timbers, overwhelming pumps at first. Emergency repairs slow influx but continuous double-watch pumping barely keeps pace.

July 19. Ship settling slowly by stern. No longer possible to steer or manoeuvre.

July 20. No further settling overnight, but vessel drifting out of control and crew exhausted. Preparations to abandon ship and take to boats.

July 21. Gathering storm driving ship on to visible reef and preventing safe launch of boats.

July 24. This is no longer the log of the Lindisfarne, the ship being lost, driven on to reef and pounded to pieces by heavy surf.

Crew took to boats in darkness. Two boats swamped immediately. No survivors. Contact lost with other boats until dawn, when Thomas Murphy's boat seen afar to capsize. Daniels and Duggan rescued but moribund, Murphy brought aboard still speaking enough to ask for his Bible. Overloaded boat driven onto uncharted beach, much patrolled by ice bear. Camp made and fire started with wreckage.

July 26 Daniels and Duggan expired during first night ashore. Murphy lingered another night and a day, then passed peacefully.

July 28. Lost crewmen buried under cairn N end of beach. Surviving crew of seven resolve attempt walk south to safety, all but essential items abandoned, including log.

If pray God we survive, we can tell our tale well enough ourselves. If we do not, and others chance upon our broken boat on this desolate beach, our log-book must tell it for us. Like gallant Thomas Murphy, we hope for better things, in this life or the next.

Joshua closed the book and looked around. For some time now he had been reading by the grey light of dawn. Simva's brand smouldered at his feet and she lay curled up in the lifeboat's bows, fast asleep. The fire was almost out. Joshua piled more wood upon it, and when he was sure it had caught, he set off along the base of the cliff, toward the north, not bothered now about bears.

The cairn was not far off: a low mound of stones piled against the cliff and topped by a crude cross fashioned from wreck-wood, which bore the simple words: *Here lie brave men*.

Joshua knelt before it for a long time. He was totally numb inside, not knowing what to think or say or do. Eventually the weight of the compass strap around his bowed neck broke into his awareness. He stood up, slipped it over his head, and hung it round the cross. '*Spero meliora*' he whispered. He saw no better things to hope for now. Only then, and only briefly, did he weep, but it was enough to waken Simva. She knew well enough to do no more than watch from afar and wait in silence until he was ready. When at length he returned to the boat in the gathering light, she stood up, clutching the heavy log-book. She didn't notice the tattered scraps of paper which fell from its pages, but Joshua did. He picked them up and smoothed them out, and read again.

The first paper was a fragment of print. Joshua

puzzled over it a while, then read it aloud:

> He giveth snow like wool:
>> and scattereth the hoarfrost like ashes.
> He casteth forth his ice like morsels:
>> who is able to abide his frost?

The second was the flyleaf from the Bible, bearing the stamp of the village church near Flint's farm. It was the very volume Joshua had left on his father's bunk two years before. As well as the stamp, it bore spidered pencil writing which was hard to decipher. Joshua read, haltingly, and this time to himself:

> *Message to my son:*
> *It may seem a sacrilege to deface a holy book as I have done. But this book cannot save me now, and I send the rest of it with my surviving crewmates, who have more need of it than I. I have no way of knowing if this message, or that I send with them, will ever find you, Joshua – but now that I have failed to save myself as I failed to save my ship, and before her, your mother, I must bid you farewell. I loved and love you more than ever I showed, and will always regret it was that love which drove me north to this awful*

place, where we must be sundered. I grow
very cold, and think my time for regret is now
short. You are young, with a long life ahead:
and if I have one last wish it is to hope that
you find it filled with better things than I
could ever bring you, though Lord knows I
tried.
Your loving father,
Thomas Murphy, Specksioneer

Joshua stood up, and pocketed the papers. He
was dry-eyed now, for he had done with tears,
and he set off along the beach, heading south,
Simva in silent pursuit.

Words whirled through Joshua's mind, none
escaped his mouth, though he wanted to scream
and shout. Wisely's bitterly prophetic curse, '*You
will find your father, boy, but you will wish you had
not,*' echoed in his ears from an Orkney beach.
But at least, and at last, he was relieved of the
gnawing uncertainty that had travelled with him
this last year. Terrible though the truth might be,
it was almost a mercy now to know it, and he
found solace in pride at his father's prowess and
courage. Joshua knew he had found within
himself the makings of a hunter and a seaman,
and was proud that it was he who had found his
father's message, and not the message him. But

he could only hope that he might measure up in bravery when tested some day: and tested he would surely be, though he hoped never as severely as this.

Chapter 36

Knowledge of the *Lindisfarne*'s fate spurred Joshua into ever-greater haste to return to the *Aurora*. He was determined that she should be freed, whatever it cost him. Soon he was running, but it was only Simva's panting breaths that told him this. She was as keen as him to find the dogs, though for different reasons, and both sighed in relief to hear barking, even before they rounded the headland behind which the dog-team sheltered.

The dogs were as excited in their greetings as always, indicating in an instant that they had been untroubled by bears, and the worst they had suffered was hunger and boredom. Simva quickly hitched the sledge, and within minutes she and Joshua were flying over the sea ice, in the wake of pattering paws and yowls of dog joy.

Simva had no wish to intrude on Joshua's thoughts, and without asking made straight for the *Aurora*, her mast tops dimly distant. Joshua spoke out at once. 'Iu, iu!' he said, more to Simva than the dogs, but they swung away nonetheless. Simva cast a puzzled glance at him. There was a pause before he spoke. 'See . . . water.' They were the first few words he'd uttered in hours, but enough to tell her he wanted to see up close the lead they'd spotted from the mountain: to make sure it had not closed up, that it would be wide enough, and above all to see how closely it approached the ship.

They soon found it, and after running alongside for a mile or so Joshua's hopes began to rise. But when he looked up for the ship's masts, to gauge the distance, he saw nothing. He stared about as the sledge hissed on another half mile, before he realised that the line of sight was blocked by pressure ridges and embedded icebergs – among them, perhaps, the one he had climbed after the williwaw hit. And if he couldn't see the *Aurora*, then no one aboard could see this lead, even from the crow's nest.

The lead ended in a blunt bay abutting a

pressure ridge. Joshua called the dogs to a halt, swung off the sledge, and scrambled up the broken ice of the ridge. The *Aurora* lay not far beyond, wearing a forlorn air of abandonment. Joshua returned to the sledge, took the harness from the lead dog, and set off, dragging the sledge up the ridge. The dogs were puzzled, until urged into effort by Simva, and with all of them pulling, they soon crested the rise with the paralysed ship in full view.

As they sped across the remaining ice Joshua whistled and hallooed, but met no response, and no sign of life. They halted the sledge near the bows. Joshua dismounted and climbed a rope ladder slung from the port side, hallooing as he rose. As he reached halfway up, two heads appeared over the rail. ' 'Ey-up lad,' said Bob Barrow. 'All right?'

Joshua kept climbing silently.

'Return on t' prodigal son,' said the other head, in Nathaniel Bridges' gruff tones.

Joshua swung over the rail and on to the deck, and still said nothing.

'But he ain't brought back his tongue to tell where he's been while his shipmates have been driven to sledge away, leavin' me and thee, Bob Barrow, to watch for 'im and bring 'im after.'

By way of reply, Joshua pulled his anorak over

his head. His rapidly disintegrating guernsey almost fell off his shoulders as he turned and bared his back. He knew the wounds looked worse than they were, and still as nothing compared to the wounds he bore within. He heard the sucking in of breath behind him with a grim satisfaction.

'Bears?'

'Aye. Well, one bear any road. And one's enough.'

'You've been lucky, lad.'

Joshua didn't feel lucky right now. He turned to face them. 'Mr Bridge. Mr Barrow. We've hastened back here to free t' ship. Storm's opened a lead up from t' north to right nearby.' He pointed with his naked arm. 'We can cut her out.'

Bob Barrow shook his head. ' 'Fraid not lad. She's fast, and us three could never cut yon ice. Me and Nathaniel only stayed to wait on you. We've all given up on t' vessel. If we set off now we can be with rest on t' ship's company by nightfall.'

Joshua summoned all his will. 'I'll not leave this ship!' he shouted. 'She's a hundred yards from freedom and I will stay aboard as many winters as I must till she finds it!'

Bob Barrow was stunned. There was a new strength about Joshua, and he chose not to

322

oppose it. 'All right son. Why don't you show me this lead o' yourn. I saw none from t' crow's nest, an' Lord knows I've been up there often enough, lookin' for you.'

Minutes later Bob Barrow stood beside Joshua, atop the pressure ridge, looking down on the still widening lead, while Simva tended the ravenous dogs. Nathaniel Bridge, who could not fit on the sledge, was thawing strips of seal meat in the Aurora's galley, as a dog reward.

Bob Barrow turned to Joshua. 'I believe you're right, lad. 'Tis possible. But we are not enough.'

'Then we will get the crew back. We'll put the bears to work if we have to. She will get free, Mr Barrow. She must.'

They returned to the ship, where the dogs devoured the still half-frozen meat Nathaniel Bridge tossed their way. Bob Barrow was making plans. 'You and t' Eskimo girl will sled off and summon crew, Joshua, while me and –'

'I told you before. I will not leave this ship. Simva can take Mr Bridge to summon Captain and crew. They will believe him more than they would me. Did you not doubt, till you saw with your own eyes? Thee and me will set to work with ice saws and whatever else.'

The dogs objected to working so soon after

food, but Simva's skills soon had them harnessed and away. Nathaniel Bridge, who had not sledded before, clung on with white knuckles and a grim face as the sledge sped away south. He was nearly spilled from the sledge as Simva took a sharp turn east, away from the course they had intended for her, but Joshua and Bob Barrow were too busy lowering huge saws to the ice to notice.

Chapter 37

'It's no good.' Bob Barrow wiped the sweat from his face and put down the ice saw. 'We can't begin it here. We must get open water *between* t' ship and this ridge.' He sat down for a much-needed rest. But his mind took no ease, for in an instant he leapt up again. 'Ash!' he cried. 'We must spread t' galley ash. There's enough sun yet to make it tell.'

He lead a doubting Joshua back to the ship, and then on trip after back-breaking trip, laden with sacks of ash and coal-dust from the galley-stove, which they scattered across the ice to make a grey-black path, as if to tempt their ship towards the open water. Eventually Bob Barrow explained. 'The darkness soaks up t' sun's scant warmth, son, to melt ice beneath, if we're lucky. But we must do more.'

Next they lugged logs and kindling, from the galley tinder store, and laid a bonfire where the ice looked thinnest. It was a struggle to light, but when it had taken, and all the spare lumber was piled nearby, they returned to their labour with ice saws. If there was any tiredness in Joshua's bones he banished it, through an effort of will. He would *not* give up.

In one of their few short breaks Bob Barrow broached the subject of his absence again. 'So what about that bear?'

Joshua shrugged. 'If he'd been right-handed he would have had me,' he shrugged, as he took up the ice saw again.

They laboured on in silence, making little progress, and breaking off every once in a while to tend the bonfire or spread more ash. Bob Barrow handed out biscuit and hunks of bread as sustenance, washed down with sips of grog from his flask, for which Joshua displayed a new-found eagerness.

Not long after noon a sudden shadow fell across the ice where they cut. Startled, both looked up, to see a line of men, Inuit and *iuksir*, arrayed along the ridge behind them.

The captain's familiar voice rang out. 'Well well, young Murphy. We may save her yet. If you can escape the clutches of a bear we can free our ship from this embrace of ice.'

Donald Lewis stepped down to Joshua's side. 'Here, lad. I'll take your place for a while.'

Other crewmen stepped down too, with ice saws, and picks, and axes, and set to work. The Inuit watched awhile, till Simva's father hefted his axe, and began attacking the ice, at which they all joined in too. Joshua looked among them in vain for Simva, till Nathaniel Bridge led him gently away, and he found himself atop the pressure ridge, alongside the captain, looking back toward the ship. Little groups of Inuit and sailors were hard at work all along the ash path to the ship herself.

The captain watched and waited while Joshua took this in, choosing his moment before he spoke, with as much gentleness as he could muster. 'I'm sorry for your loss, Joshua. We all are.' He indicated the *Lindisfarne*'s log, tucked under his arm. 'We all know the story. Your Inuit lass gave Mr Bridge this log on the way to her camp.'

Joshua frowned. That wasn't the plan.

'Aye, lad. That's why we're here so soon. She went straight to her camp, ignoring you and Mr

Bridge alike. Her kin hitched dog-sleds and raced out to collect those of us you see here arrayed. The rest of the crew follow on, manhauling our clumsy vehicles.' He paused. 'I am astonished at the speed of those dogs.'

'But where is she?'

'Your lass? She stayed at camp, exhausted and hungry and fairly played out by climbing mountains, not to mention nights in upturned lifeboats and encounters with fearsome beasts. She needed food and warmth and rest, son. She's tough, but not as tough as you.'

Oh yes she is, thought Joshua. He said nothing, but still could not understand why she had not returned.

'And you need food too. Back on board the cook is brewing broth. If you've left him any tinder, that is. First bowl to you, then straight back here, eh?' Joshua set off, but the captain called him back. 'I am truly sorry for the loss of your father, Joshua. I mourn him with you. He was a good sailor, and a fine man.' He tapped the log. 'And from this account, I see where you derive your courage. I know you are grieving now, and I wish no answer till you are ready: but I reaffirm my offer that you join my crew.'

Joshua stared at him. 'To have a crew you must first have a ship, Captain.' He took up a pick and made for the ridge. 'I have no appetite for broth.'

The sun began to drop from its zenith as the work went on. Joshua was everywhere: ferrying broth and bread, oiling ice saws, tending the fire, spreading ash; and, when his dwindling energy permitted, hacking at the ice with whatever came to hand. All knew of his loss, even the Inuit, but none spoke of it.

With so many willing hands they made much better progress, and a great shout went up when clear water appeared at the halfway point. The fire had already been split into two smaller blazes, one nearer the ship and the other off towards the ridge. A new enthusiasm for ice sawing took hold at the fresh edges of the pool where the fire had been. A channel quickly extended in opposite directions from this bonfire pool, towards the two places where the ice retained its stubborn resistance – around the ship, and at the ridge.

The work was mainly conducted in silence, apart from flashes of Yorkshire banter, or the Inuit equivalent. Occasionally there was a brief and tuneless snatch of song, but for the most part the only music was provided by the tapping of the picks and the rasp of the ice saws.

Every time Joshua looked up to ease his aching back, he hunted about for Simva's face, even though he knew she would not be there. When the sledge party returned he searched among them too, though none of them were Inuit. Disappointment at her absence was soon compensated, as more and more ice was cut away, and the channels extended rapidly outwards.

Work now concentrated around the ship and at the ridge, but, after the rapid lengthening of the channels, the snail's pace progress in these two sites dampened spirits. The captain sensed this, and, fearing that nightfall might undo all their efforts, he called Mr Colbeck and Mr Hobbs aside. 'Enough of this pick work, gentlemen. Let's sally ship.'

Chapter 38

The crew and the Inuit were assembled on deck in a huddled mass. First the captain had them cram together on the port rail, and then at his command, run in a body to the starboard side, and back. This they did repeatedly, to ominous sounds from below deck and the surface of the ice. As soon as they felt a hint of movement, the captain had them all run from bow to stern and back. Several Inuit and one or two crew went sprawling, bashing shins on hatch covers and bumping into capstans. When Nathaniel Bridge fell into the hold, the panting breaths were broken by laughter, which doubled once they were sure he was uninjured. Even Joshua joined in.

The movement of the ship increased further, but was still minimal. After a brief halt the captain spaced the crew and Inuit around the deck and had them jump up and down in time to his commands. This produced much noise though little result, but when they ran on the spot in time, there was a sudden lurch, an enormous cracking noise, and a shout of triumph from old Benjamin Watt, observing on the ice below. 'She's almost there!' he yelled. 'Just a little more, sir!'

'Now, my lads,' called the captain. 'Back to port. Quickly mind. Ready . . . Go! Starboard! . . . Port! . . . Starboard! . . . Port! . . .' Joshua hurled himself back and forth across the deck. At each side he hung out over the ice, desperate to see what was happening below. There was another sudden lurch, and a louder crack than before, and this time the feeling underfoot told them she was afloat again at last. She rolled gently back and forth, as if breasting a light North Sea swell, and when Joshua looked up he saw her mast heads tracing familiar arcs across the Greenland skies. There was a huge cheer.

'Well done lads, well done indeed. We'll get out of here and home yet, so we will. Now every man jack back to yonder ridge, with efforts a-doubled. Mr Colbeck! Break out the grog!'

But even grog-fuelled efforts made little impact on the solid ice of the pressure ridge. Hours of hacking had taken it down to somewhere near the waterline, but there was no way of telling how much ice lay below. The lengthening shadows and the way the sweat chilled told all too clearly that the day was dying, and with it perhaps the last of their hopes.

The captain looked up to assess the rising wind, then called port watch back to the ship. Joshua went along too, even though he was a starboard man. 'We'll lay out ice anchors to hold her, Mr Colbeck, while we loose aloft every scrap of canvas we possess,' the captain declared. 'We will use this wind to ram our way out.'

Joshua leapt up the rigging with the rest of the men and unfurled sail after sail. He felt the ship begin to strain against the ice anchors, as if she were eager to move after her long captivity. When every sail was sheeted in and the wind at its peak, the captain signalled the anchors let go. The *Aurora* leapt forward like a horse bolting from its stable, shouldering aside the chunks of ice they had cut away as she gathered pace up the channel.

'All hands astern!' The captain wanted his crew as far from the impact as possible, and needed the weight there to raise the bows. Mr

Hobbs and Mr Colbeck blew furiously on bosun's whistles to warn the starboard watch and the Inuit, still hacking at the ridge. They sprang aside as the ship galloped up.

'Brace!'

Joshua clung to the starboard ratlines and scanned the anxious faces about him.

Edward Sumner crossed himself. 'She's not built for this,' he muttered.

'Maybe not,' said Donald Lewis. 'But she will break through or break up trying. One thing for sure: we'll only get one go.'

The impact was stunning. Joshua's grip was wrenched from the ratlines and he was flung headlong forward. Above him the masts shuddered and strained, and a yard arm crashed to the empty foredeck in a tangle of sails and rigging. The sounds of crunching ice and shrieking timber filled the air. The bows rode up and up before she stopped. The ridge creaked and groaned: but it did not give.

A shocked silence followed, in which men picked themselves up and peered over the rail. 'Taking water below, sir!' called Nathaniel Bridge, who had stayed in the hold to watch for leaks. Two men dropped down to help him in repair work, while others took to the pumps.

The captain folded his arms. 'We will warp

her back and go again,' he said.

A worried murmur rippled around the crew. 'She will surely be stove in before yon ice will yield,' said Edward Sumner. Some heads nodded in agreement.

The captain jumped up on to a hatch-cover to make himself seen and heard. 'Aye men, I know, we risk our ship. But did we not abandon her, to my eternal shame? All of us, except this lad here and the two who volunteered to wait for him, a whole winter if need be, gave her up for dead.'

Joshua glanced at Bob Barrow, who would not meet his eye. He had had no idea.

The captain continued. 'We owe her, and him, another effort. And if she is stove, then what have we lost we did not already give away? We will go again.'

The sails were furled, the yard arm cut free, and the ship warped backwards using capstans and ice anchors. As she slid off the ridge there were more shouts about leaks from below, and the hold rang with hammering as emergency battens were fitted. Foot by foot she was hauled back to her winter stable and secured there once more with ice anchors while the canvas was lowered.

With everyone aboard, the captain set her free again. The ship's company and the Inuit huddled close together, as far astern as they could get, while the captain clung to the foremast, signalling to the helmsman where to strike. He craned his neck back and roared into the wind and the sails above him as the ship approached the forbidding wall of ice. 'Blow, damn you, blow! And blow again! Faster, I say! I WANT MORE SPEED!'

The impact was even more violent than the first. Cries of pain from the men tumbling over him mingled with the ship's shrieks in Joshua's ears. But they mingled too with a cracking sound as the bows rode up the ridge.

'Now, men! All hands forward!' They raced to the bows to increase the weight on the splintering ice, all except Edward Sumner, who writhed in pain, blood pouring from a leg wound.

The ridge gave, not so much with a crack as a slowly sinking surge. Broken chunks of ice surfaced violently in the open waters of the lead, to bang against the descending bows. The noise was tremendous. After a final lurch she was free, bobbing in the seething waters of the lead, proud to be a ship once more.

A enormous cheer went up and echoed back from the mountains, and there was much shaking of hands and slapping of backs, and even rubbing of noses.

'Grog, men! And double grog!' shouted the captain. As his crew toasted their freedom he dropped into the hold to inspect the damage. The celebration stilled, but the hammering did not, while the anxious sailors awaited his return. When he came back up it was with a smile. 'She leaks, 'tis true, but we can stem it well enough. Let's go home!'

The Inuit left the deck, climbing down the ladder one by one, amid farewells and beams of gratitude. The last to go was Simva's father. Joshua stood by as he took his leave. The captain shook his hand and pointed to the still-laden sledges, which there had been no time to unload. 'A thousand thanks, sir, to you and your kin. We owe you our ship, and perhaps our lives. Please take our stores yonder, not as payment, but as gift in return.' Simva's father smiled.

Joshua turned to him as he swung over the rail and on to the ladder. 'Please pass my farewell to Simva, sir,' was all he could find to say. Simva's father nodded at him, smiled again, and dropped out of sight into the deepening twilight.

A three-quarter moon rose beyond the mountains as the Inuit returned to their sledges.

'We'll leave at once, gentlemen,' the captain commanded, as the crew busied themselves cheerily about him. 'Both watches on deck.'

Chapter 39

Joshua took to his crow's nest. His ship might be free but his spirit was not, and he did not want to mingle with the uncomplicated joy of his crewmates while he mourned all his losses. He curled up inside his refuge, where exhaustion outweighed his grief enough to bring him sleep.

He was not sure how much time had passed before the motion of the ship woke him, but it was now dark. He could not stay curled up for long, surrounded as he was by the fresh smell of salt water, the snap of the sails below and the creak of the rigging; all the well-remembered sounds and sensations of a ship under way.

He stood up and peered over the barrel lip.

The rising moon cast a glittering path for the ship to follow as she threaded her way along the lead, and towards a confusing choice of channels. A seal lazily cruised along ahead of them. Moonlight flashed repeatedly to left and right of the seal in a steady rhythm. Joshua stared, trying to make it out, and when he was sure that this was no seal at all, he leapt out of his barrel and raced to the deck, where he ran the length of the slippery bowsprit.

There below, paddling along in her kayak, was a smiling Simva. She dropped back to surf the *Aurora*'s bow wave in her frail craft, and laughed up at him. He waved back, warmly reflecting her smile.

As they drew near the three channels ahead, she paddled on, and without hesitation took the westernmost. It was not until then that Joshua realised Simva had not rested at all. She had taken to the kayak the moment she reached her camp, and had spent the day navigating the channels so that she could lead the *Aurora* to the open sea. She had never lost faith that Joshua would free his ship and need her as his guide.

The grateful helmsman followed the tiny kayak through a twisting moonlit maze. Walrus watched them glide by, seals blew in the water all around, and Joshua even fancied he saw a narwhal, with healing wounds in its side, as the northern lights flickered behind the mountains. Soon they needed no more guiding, for the open sea lay ahead. Simva slipped back to paddle alongside, as the ship lifted to the swell.

She waved her paddles, between strokes, while Joshua waved back with his whole body. Neither of them spoke. As the ship gathered speed and Simva dropped back, Joshua walked the length of the rail to the very stern. He watched and waved till the flashing paddles had long gone. 'I'll come back,' he called after her. 'I *will* come back.'

The captain spoke to him from the helm. Joshua didn't need to look to know they were going south. 'She points only one way now, Joshua. Home.'

Joshua shook his head. Much though he would love to see Emmy and Nelson again, he had no home in Whitby or anywhere else in England. And he could never now be fully at home in the north, knowing what it had done to his father, who would lie here for ever under ice and stone, with drowned crewmates for company and prowling bears to keep his grave. Without thinking where he had left it, he reached up to his neck for his compass, but touched instead the charm Simva had hung there after she'd saved his life. His other hand slipped into his pocket, and felt his scrimshaw and the tattered pages torn from his father's Bible. Apart from the ragged clothes he stood in, these things were all he had in the world: but they were more precious than jewels.

Joshua looked ahead, along the length of the battered ship he had done so much to save. A flag fluttered proudly at his shoulder. Her bows sliced the moon-path in twain, her silver sails puffed out, and above them her mast-tops swung past spangly stars. Joshua knew then, as certainly as he knew where north was, that the only home he'd ever have was on the deck of a ship, at sea.

If you enjoyed

why not try

Hunting Gumnor
by Stephen Potts

*Shortlisted for the Branford Boase
Award for first novels*

> *'All the best things are like that.
> Only there for a moment. As soon
> as you want them, they disappear'*
> *'No they're not,'* Rarty argued. *'Gumnor.
> She didn't change. She was always there,
> the same. She's the best thing.'*

But Gumnor, the last sea creature of
her kind, has vanished. The port has lost its
foghorn and Rarty's family their home.
Why has Gumnor gone away?

An enchanting quest, a timeless story
of the sea and those who live by it.

*'evocative and atmospheric, capturing the
sound and taste of the sea . . . an exciting
yarn with a surprise ending'*
TES

TOMMY
TROUBLE

*'What's the trouble, Tommy? Can't read?
Can't write? Or just can't be bothered?'*

At school everyone jeers at Tommy
because his reading and writing aren't good.

But there's one thing he *can* read, and his
struggle to understand it wins him the
friendship of old soldier Jack.

When Jack goes away, Tommy is shattered.
His father has already gone: who will desert
him next? It would be so easy to give up.

But Tommy's not the type
to surrender . . .

*'Beautifully written . . . This is a warm,
rich and rewarding read'*
Books for Keeps

The Wind Singer

by William Nicholson

Winner of the Smarties Prize

*'I hate school! I hate ratings! I won't reach higher!
I won't strive harder! I won't make tomorrow better
than today! Pongo to exams!'*

In the walled city state of Aramanth, exams are
everything. When Kestrel Hath dares to rebel,
the Chief Examiner humiliates her father and
sentences the whole family to the harshest
punishment. Desperate to save them,
Kestrel learns the secret of the wind singer,
and she and her twin brother, Bowman,
set out on a terrifying journey to the true
source of the evil that grips Aramanth.

*'a gripping read . . . a beautifully narrated,
warm thriller of a book, full of inventiveness,
action and passion.'*
Guardian

*'In terms of imagination and sheer scale,
it's as ambitious as books get . . . think
Star Wars and then some'*
Daily Telegraph

Kensuke's Kingdom

by MICHAEL MORPURGO

Winner of the Children's Book Award

'I heard the wind above me in the sails. I remember thinking, this is silly, you haven't got your safety harness on, you haven't got your lifejacket on. You shouldn't be doing this. Then the boat veered violently and I was thrown sideways. I had no time to grab the guard-rail. I was in the cold of the sea before I could even open my mouth to scream.'

Washed up on an island in the Pacific, Michael struggles to survive on his own. He can't find food, he can't find water. In the end, he curls up to die. When he wakes, there is a plate beside him of fish, of fruit, and a bowl of fresh water. He is not alone . . .

'A magnificent contemporary odyssey:
a beautifully written account of a boy's
voyage of discovery.'
TES

'Exciting and thought-provoking'
Observer